TRISTYN BARBERI

City Of Sorrow

Neon Shadows Duology

First published by TB Press 2025

Copyright © 2025 by Tristyn Barberi

All rights reserved. No part of this publication may be reproduced, stored or transmitted in any form or by any means, electronic, mechanical, photocopying, recording, scanning, or otherwise without written permission from the publisher. It is illegal to copy this book, post it to a website, or distribute it by any other means without permission.

This novel is entirely a work of fiction. The names, characters and incidents portrayed in it are the work of the author's imagination. Any resemblance to actual persons, living or dead, events or localities is entirely coincidental.

First edition

This book was professionally typeset on Reedsy. Find out more at reedsy.com

Contents

Chapter 1	1
Chapter 2	6
Chapter 3	11
Chapter 4	14
Chapter 5	17
Chapter 6	20
Chapter 7	23
Chapter 8	26
Chapter 9	29
Chapter 10	32
Chapter 11	35
Chapter 12	38
Chapter 13	41
Chapter 14	44
Chapter 15	48
Chapter 16	51
Chapter 17	54
Chapter 18	57
Chapter 19	60
Chapter 20	63
Chapter 21	66
Chapter 22	69 .
Chapter 23	72
Chapter 24	75

Chapter 25	78
Chapter 26	81
Chapter 27	83
Chapter 28	86
Chapter 29	89
Chapter 30	92
Chapter 31	95
Chapter 32	98
Chapter 33	100
Chapter 34	102
Chapter 35	105
Chapter 36	107
Chapter 37	110
Chapter 38	113
Chapter 39	116
Chapter 40	119
Chapter 41	121
Chapter 42	124
Chapter 43	126
Chapter 44	131
Chapter 45	134
About The Author	136
Also By Tristyn Barberi	137

Chapter 1

The harsh white light of the Network lab seared Anya's eyelids, even through the thin film of her closed eyes. A dull, persistent throb pulsed behind her temples, a constant reminder of the Chrysalis's violent demise. Fragments of memory flickered like broken neon signs in the darkness behind her lids.

Griffin's pale face in the transport... the sleek black vehicles descending like silent predators... the searing blue energy... the roar of the collapsing tower... darkness.

Each shard of recollection brought with it a fresh wave of pain – the phantom ache of her crushed shoulder, the lingering fear for Griffin's safety, the bitter taste of betrayal by the very organization she had once believed in.

She was still strapped to the cold medical bed, the reinforced restraints digging into her wrists and ankles. The sterile scent of antiseptic and ozone filled her nostrils, a constant testament to her captivity. The rhythmic hum of the Network's machinery was the only soundtrack to her confinement, a monotonous drone that amplified the silence of her defiance.

Days? Weeks? Time had become a meaningless blur within these walls. The tests continued, a relentless assault on her mind and body. Cold probes against her skin, the invasive pressure of the neural scanners, the draining energy siphoned from her link to the Spire device. Each session left her weakened, her resolve frayed, but her spirit unbroken.

Silas's face would occasionally loom above her, his voice a carefully modulated blend of persuasion and threat. He would reiterate his bargain – cooperation for her family's safety. He would show her fleeting glimpses of Elena and Misha on monitors, carefully curated images designed to break her resistance. But Anya saw the cold calculation in his eyes, the hunger for the Spire's power, and her distrust remained a solid wall.

Whisper's determined face as she covered their escape... Jax's grim satisfaction as the Chrysalis crumbled... Boris's roar as the transport sped away...

The faces of her fledgling syndicate flashed in her mind, a fragile beacon of hope in this sterile darkness. Had they escaped? Were they still out there, fighting? The uncertainty was a constant torment.

The memory of her realization, the chilling thought that the Network could track others like her, resurfaced with a renewed urgency. The faint blue resonance of the Spire device within her felt like a beacon, a potential target for the very technology that now held her captive. But the image of crushing that tracking device under her boot in the chaos of the tower's fall brought a small, fierce spark of satisfaction. They wouldn't track *her* that easily again.

As another set of Network personnel approached her bed, their movements precise and devoid of emotion, Anya closed her eyes again, feigning unconsciousness. Let them think her broken. Let them underestimate her. Beneath the surface of her enforced stillness, a new resolve was hardening. She would endure. She would remember. And when the opportunity arose, she would make them pay for every moment of her captivity, for every lie, for every life they had twisted in pursuit of their terrifying vision. The echoes of the past were a painful reminder of what she had lost, but they also fueled the burning desire for a future where the Network's control was shattered.

The charade of unconsciousness didn't last long. The Network's methods were thorough, their patience limited. A sharp prick in her arm and the familiar rush of a stimulant forced Anya back to full awareness. Silas stood at the foot of her bed, his expression impatient.

"Enough games, Anya," he said, his voice hard. "We have... observed your unique connection. Now, we require practical demonstrations. Under controlled conditions, of course."

Two armed guards flanked her bed as the restraints were released, replaced by energy cuffs that pulsed with a low, threatening hum. Anya's muscles screamed in protest as she was forced to sit up, the world swaying momentarily.

They led her to a large, sterile testing chamber. Network scientists peered from behind thick observation glass, their faces illuminated by the glow of their monitors. In the center of the chamber was a series of obstacles: energy fields flickering with lethal potential, moving targets that reacted with surprising speed, and pressure plates that triggered sonic bursts.

"Your task is simple, Anya," Silas announced, his voice echoing through the chamber's intercom. "Navigate the course. Use... your abilities. We wish to quantify your limits, understand the parameters of your... resonance."

Anya's jaw tightened. This wasn't about understanding her limits; it was about understanding the Spire device, about dissecting her connection to it so they could replicate its power. She clenched her fists, a surge of defiance rising within her. She wouldn't give them what they wanted easily.

The energy cuffs pulsed again, a sharp reminder of her captivity. Reluctantly, Anya stepped onto the testing floor. The first energy field flickered before her, a shimmering barrier of lethal energy. Instinct screamed at her to activate the Spire device, to feel its familiar warmth and the surge of power that would allow her to perceive the field's fluctuations, to slip through its gaps.

But she resisted. She moved cautiously, relying on her agility and the reflexes honed by her Network training. She studied the field's pattern, the subtle shifts in its energy, and with a burst of speed, dodged through a momentary lull.

The moving targets were next, darting across the chamber with unnerving speed. Again, the urge to tap into the device was strong. With it, she could anticipate their movements, perceive their trajectories with effortless precision. Instead, she relied on her natural reflexes, her movements less fluid, less certain, but still effective. She managed to tag a few targets with the deactivated energy pistol they had begrudgingly given her.

The pressure plates were the most challenging. Invisible to the naked eye, they triggered disorienting sonic bursts that threatened to incapacitate her. Anya moved with painstaking slowness, her senses straining for any subtle change in the floor's texture, any telltale shimmer in the air. She triggered several bursts, the sonic waves slamming into her, disorienting her, but she pressed on, refusing to yield.

Throughout the tests, Anya could feel the intense scrutiny from behind the observation glass. Their gazes were like physical probes, dissecting her movements, analyzing her struggles. Silas watched with a cold intensity, his frustration growing with each instance she refrained from fully utilizing her abilities.

CHAPTER 1

"You're holding back, Anya," his voice echoed through the chamber. "Don't be foolish. Cooperation will make this... less unpleasant."

Anya ignored him, her focus solely on navigating the treacherous course. She stumbled, she faltered, she felt the limitations of her unaided human form acutely. But with every deliberate movement, every resisted urge to unleash the Spire's power, she felt a small sense of victory. She was denying them the full spectacle of her abilities, forcing them to rely on incomplete data, obscuring the true nature of her connection to the device. The cage of the testing chamber might hold her body, but her will, and the secrets of her power, remained stubbornly her own.

Chapter 2

In the dimly lit confines of their new, temporary hideout – a repurposed shipping container in the sprawling docks district – Whisper traced holographic schematics of the Network facility where Anya was being held. Boris, his massive frame casting long shadows in the flickering emergency light, meticulously cleaned his scavenged heavy weaponry. Jax, hunched over a datapad, muttered strings of code as he attempted to penetrate the Network's formidable security systems.

The atmosphere was thick with a tense blend of worry and grim determination. Anya's capture had been a brutal blow, a stark reminder of the Network's reach and ruthlessness. Their priority now was clear: get her back.

"Their security around this 'Chrysalis Mark II' is tighter than a synth-steel drum," Jax grumbled, running a hand through his perpetually disheveled hair. "They've learned from the first one. No easy backdoors."

Boris grunted in agreement. "Direct assault? Suicide. They'll be expecting that."

Whisper zoomed in on a section of the schematic, her cybernetic eyes scanning for vulnerabilities. "They're focused on external threats. Anya's capture likely reinforced their internal security, but their perimeter is still their primary concern."

CHAPTER 2

"So, how do we get in?" Boris asked, his gaze steady.

Whisper tapped a specific access point on the schematic – a heavily guarded loading dock on the facility's west side. "Diversion. We hit them hard, draw their forces to the perimeter. While they're occupied, a small team slips in."

"Small and quiet," Jax added, his fingers still flying across the datapad. "I might be able to create a localized blackout in a specific sector, give them a window."

The planning continued, each member contributing their expertise. But beneath the surface of their focused efforts, a subtle tension lingered around Jax. Whisper's internal investigations, running in the background of their rescue preparations for months now, had unearthed a disturbing piece of information.

Months ago, when Anya had first come to Jax, seeking information about unusual energy signatures and pre-Network tech – the very search that had inadvertently led the Network to her and the Spire device – Jax had logged that query. Standard procedure, he'd claimed. But the timing of the Network's intensified search, the precision with which they had targeted Anya weeks later... it felt too convenient.

Whisper had cross-referenced Jax's logs with known Network surveillance patterns and internal communications intercepts over the past few months. The data painted a damning picture. A ping, originating from Jax's terminal shortly after Anya's visit, had coincided with a significant uptick in Network activity in Anya's sector. A subtle flag, easily missed in the deluge of data, but a flag nonetheless.

She watched Jax, his brow furrowed in concentration, a familiar knot of suspicion tightening in her chest. Had he been compromised months ago? Had he unknowingly – or knowingly – led the Network to Anya? The thought was a bitter poison, threatening to fracture their fragile alliance.

Now, as they planned Anya's rescue, the stakes were even higher. Could they trust Jax implicitly? Or was he a potential mole, a blind spot that the Network could exploit?

Whisper made a mental note to confront him, but not yet. Not when Anya's life hung in the balance. For now, she would compartmentalize her doubts, focusing on the immediate goal. But the seed of suspicion had been planted months ago, a dark undercurrent beneath their desperate efforts to bring Anya home. The rescue plan was taking shape, but the foundation of their trust had begun to crack long before.

Silas led Anya through a sterile corridor, the hum of unseen machinery a constant companion. The energy cuffs on her wrists pulsed faintly, a persistent reminder of her captivity. He stopped before a reinforced observation window, the transparent barrier thick enough to withstand significant force.

"I wanted to show you... our progress, Anya," Silas said, his voice laced with a disturbing blend of pride and clinical detachment.

Beyond the window, in a vast, dimly lit chamber, lay a scene that twisted Anya's stomach. On several operating tables, under the harsh glare of surgical lamps, were grotesque figures. They were human, or at least had been. Limbs from different bodies were crudely stitched together, cybernetic implants haphazardly grafted onto flesh, and exposed neural pathways pulsed with unnatural light. It was a macabre amalgamation, a Frankensteinian nightmare cobbled together from the "donors" the Network had been collecting.

Anya recoiled, a wave of nausea rising in her throat. "What... what is this?" she choked out, her voice barely a whisper.

Silas watched her reaction with a chilling satisfaction. "This,

Anya, is the nascent stage of Project Chimera. A unification. A transcendence of individual limitations. We are learning to integrate, to combine the strengths of many into a single, more... efficient form."

The figures twitched on the tables, their movements jerky and unnatural. Some emitted guttural moans, sounds that spoke of pain and confusion. Anya's heart clenched with horror and a profound sense of violation. These weren't just donors; they were victims, their bodies desecrated in the name of Silas's twisted vision.

"You're monsters," Anya hissed, her eyes blazing with fury. "This is an abomination!"

Silas merely chuckled, a dry, humorless sound. "Sentimentality is a weakness, Anya. These are merely components, raw materials in the creation of something greater. We are pushing the boundaries of human potential."

He gestured towards one of the figures – a torso with multiple grafted arms, cybernetic eyes blinking erratically, and exposed wires snaking across its stitched flesh. "Observe. The combined strength of multiple limbs, enhanced sensory input... Imagine the possibilities, Anya. A collective consciousness housed in adaptable, enhanced vessels."

Anya's mind reeled. This wasn't the subtle neural manipulation she had initially feared. This was physical desecration, a grotesque violation of the human form. And her mother and brother... were they destined for this?

"Your mother's unique neural structure," Silas continued, his voice taking on a more clinical tone, "has provided invaluable insights into neural integration. And your brother... his resilience during the initial stages of our preliminary bonding experiments has been... promising."

Anya's blood ran cold. Preliminary bonding experiments? What had they done to Misha?

"This, Anya," Silas concluded, his gaze returning to her, "is the future. And you, with your unique connection, could be instrumental in its realization. Imagine, Anya, not just enhancing individuals, but weaving them together into a harmonious whole."

He paused, letting the horrifying image sink in. "Resist, and your family becomes part of this... evolution. Cooperate, and perhaps... perhaps they will be spared the more... direct forms of integration."

The threat hung heavy in the air, more chilling than any physical restraint. Silas had shown her the grotesque reality of Project Chimera, a horrifying glimpse into the fate that awaited her family if she failed to comply. The Frankensteinian abominations beyond the glass were a stark and brutal testament to the Network's utter disregard for human life and dignity. Anya's defiance wavered, a knot of terror tightening in her chest. The serpent's bargain had taken on a whole new, horrifying dimension.

Chapter 3

The image of the grotesque hybrids beyond the observation window haunted Anya's waking thoughts and bled into her restless sleep. Silas's veiled threat hung heavy in the sterile air, a constant reminder of the monstrous fate that could await her mother and Misha. The weight of their potential suffering pressed down on her, a crushing burden.

When Silas returned to the testing chamber, his usual cold impatience was replaced by a carefully cultivated air of understanding. "Anya," he began, his voice softer than before. "I know this is difficult. But consider the alternative. Cooperation, a willingness to show us the extent of your connection... it is the only path to ensuring your family's well-being."

Anya's jaw remained tight, her eyes narrowed with suspicion. She still didn't trust him, not an inch. But the horrifying reality of Project Chimera, the stitched-together remnants of human beings, had planted a seed of reluctant compromise in her mind. If a small demonstration of her abilities could buy her family even a sliver of protection, could she afford not to?

"What do you want me to do?" she asked, her voice low and strained, the words tasting like ash in her mouth.

Silas's lips curved into a thin, satisfied smile. "The obstacle course again. But this time, Anya, I want you to... embrace your connection. Show us the full extent of the Spire's influence."

Anya stepped onto the testing floor, the familiar obstacles looming before her. The energy fields flickered, the targets darted, the pressure plates lay hidden. This time, she didn't hesitate. With a deep breath, she focused her will, reaching for the familiar warmth that lay dormant within her.

The Spire device pulsed against her skin, and the world around her sharpened. The energy fields shimmered with intricate patterns, their fluctuations becoming clear. The targets' movements telegraphed fractions of a second before they occurred. The subtle vibrations of the pressure plates resonated through the floor.

She moved through the course with an effortless grace she had deliberately suppressed before. She flowed through the energy fields as if they were mere illusions, tagged the targets with pinpoint accuracy, and navigated the pressure plates without triggering a single sonic burst. The deactivated energy pistol felt like an extension of her will, guided by an almost precognitive awareness.

Behind the observation glass, the Network scientists murmured with excited intensity, their instruments recording every minute fluctuation in Anya's energy signature, every subtle shift in her neural activity. Silas watched with a keen focus, his eyes gleaming with a mixture of triumph and scientific curiosity. They were getting data, valuable data about the Spire's capabilities and its link to Anya's physiology.

But as the Spire device flared to life within her, a faint, almost imperceptible energy pulse radiated outwards, a subtle echo in the facility's electronic systems. Unbeknownst to Silas and his team, that pulse, a unique signature of Anya's fully activated connection, rippled through the building's infrastructure, a

CHAPTER 3

silent beacon in the electronic noise.

Miles away, in the cramped confines of their dockside hideout, Whisper sat hunched over a modified Network scanner, its display a chaotic mess of encrypted signals. She had been tirelessly searching for any trace of Anya, any anomaly in the Network's communication or energy grids.

Suddenly, a faint, distinct pattern bloomed on the screen – a brief, powerful resonance unlike anything she had encountered before. It was fleeting, almost swallowed by the surrounding static, but it was there. A familiar energy signature, amplified and unmistakable.

Whisper's cybernetic eyes widened. It was Anya. And the strength of the signal... she knew exactly where in the facility Anya was, deep within Sector Gamma, likely undergoing some kind of intensive testing.

A grim determination settled on Whisper's face. Anya had shown her hand, a calculated risk driven by desperation. Now it was their turn to act. The data Silas had gained came at a price he didn't yet realize. He had inadvertently illuminated Anya's prison, and Whisper knew, with a chilling certainty, that their rescue operation had just become a whole lot more urgent.

Chapter 4

Weeks crawled by, an endless cycle of tests and sterile confinement. Anya had walked the obstacle course countless times, each reluctant display of her abilities meticulously recorded and analyzed. Silas's demeanor had shifted, the initial impatience replaced by a smug satisfaction, believing he was finally gaining her cooperation.

Then came the unexpected summons. Two guards, their expressions impassive, led Anya through a series of sterile corridors, deeper into the facility than she had been before. A knot of apprehension tightened in her chest. Where were they taking her?

They stopped before a reinforced door, and with a soft hiss, it slid open. Anya stepped into a small, equally sterile room. And then she saw them.

Her breath hitched. Elena. Her mother looked thinner, her face etched with a weariness Anya had never seen, but her eyes, when they met Anya's, held a flicker of the familiar warmth. Relief washed over Anya, so potent it almost buckled her knees.

And then she saw Misha. He sat quietly on a small cot, his gaze distant, almost vacant. He looked physically unharmed, but there was a stillness about him that felt wrong. As Anya's eyes focused on him, she noticed something else, something that sent a fresh wave of icy dread through her.

At the base of Misha's neck, just below his hairline, a small, circular device was embedded in his skin. It pulsed with a faint, ethereal blue glow, an unsettling echo of the energy that coursed through Anya's own veins.

"Anya," Elena whispered, her voice trembling with a mixture of relief and fear. She took a hesitant step towards her daughter, but a subtle gesture from one of the guards stopped her.

"Mother," Anya choked out, her gaze fixed on the device on Misha's neck. "What... what have they done to him?"

Silas stepped into the room, a smug expression on his face. "Progress, Anya. We are exploring... alternative methods of integration. Your brother possesses a unique receptivity."

Anya's blood ran cold. The blue glow... it was the same energy. They were experimenting on Misha, using technology derived from the Spire device.

She rushed towards Misha, ignoring the guards' restraining hands. "Misha! It's me, Anya! Can you hear me?"

Misha blinked slowly, his eyes focusing on her with a delayed recognition. "Anya?" His voice was soft, almost dreamlike.

"They've done something to him," Anya said, her voice tight with fury, turning back to Silas. "What is that thing on his neck?"

"A facilitator," Silas explained smoothly. "It allows for a more... direct connection. We are learning to harmonize neural pathways."

Elena's eyes were filled with terror. "He's not himself, Anya. He's... quiet. He doesn't..." Her voice trailed off, choked with emotion.

Anya reached out, wanting to touch Misha, to tear the device from his neck, but the guards held her back firmly. The faint blue glow pulsed steadily, an insidious light illuminating the Network's cruelty.

The brief reunion was bittersweet, a fragile glimpse of family overshadowed by the horrifying reality of their captivity. Anya had seen her mother and brother, confirming they were alive, but the sight of the device on Misha's neck, pulsing with that familiar, alien energy, filled her with a chilling certainty. Their safety was a lie, a dangling carrot to ensure her continued cooperation. They weren't just being held; they were being actively experimented on, their very beings twisted for Silas's monstrous vision. The price of this fleeting reunion was a deeper understanding of the Network's depravity and a renewed surge of desperate resolve within Anya. She had to get them out, all of them, before they became nothing more than components in Silas's grotesque imitation of the future.

Chapter 5

The sight of the pulsating blue device embedded in Misha's neck, coupled with Silas's cold explanation, snapped something within Anya. The fragile hope offered by the brief reunion shattered, replaced by a white-hot rage. This wasn't about keeping them safe; it was about control, about twisting her family into instruments for their horrific agenda.

Ignoring the restraining hands of the guards, Anya lunged at Silas with a guttural cry. Years of street fighting and Network training kicked in, her movements swift and brutal. She aimed a vicious strike at his face, fueled by pure, unadulterated fury.

Silas, however, was quicker than she anticipated. He sidestepped her attack with a practiced ease, a flicker of annoyance crossing his features. Before Anya could recover her balance, his foot lashed out, catching her squarely in the ribs.

A searing pain exploded in her side, stealing her breath. Anya gasped, stumbling backward, her vision momentarily blurring. She instinctively clutched at her ribs, a sharp, agonizing spike shooting through her with every shallow breath.

Silas watched her fall, his expression hardening. "Impulsive, Anya. Emotionally driven. Such a predictable flaw."

He didn't offer her a hand up. Instead, he gestured curtly to the guards. "Secure her. Return her to the holding cell. She will remain restrained until she regains a modicum of control."

Anya lay on the cold floor, the pain in her ribs a relentless torment. She tried to get up, to fight back, but every movement sent shards of agony through her torso. The guards, their faces impassive, moved in, their grip firm and unforgiving.

"Don't touch me," Anya spat, her voice ragged, but the fight had gone out of her for now. The raw, physical pain was a stark reminder of her powerlessness within these walls.

They hauled her up roughly, ignoring her pained cries, and dragged her back through the sterile corridors. The image of Misha's vacant eyes and the pulsating blue glow on his neck burned behind her eyelids, fueling a bitter, impotent rage.

Back in the familiar confines of her holding cell, they strapped her down to the medical bed once more, the cold metal of the restraints a stark contrast to the burning ache in her side. Anya lay there, panting, each breath a painful reminder of her failed defiance.

Tears of frustration and pain welled in her eyes. She had let her anger get the better of her, and all she had accomplished was to inflict more pain upon herself and further solidify her captivity. Silas had seen her outburst, witnessed her raw emotion, and it would likely only reinforce his belief that she could be manipulated through her love for her family.

As the throbbing in her ribs slowly subsided to a dull, constant ache, a cold resolve began to form within Anya amidst the pain. Raw emotion might be a flaw, but it was also a source of strength. Silas might think he had broken her spirit, but he was wrong. She would endure this pain, she would learn from her impulsiveness, and she would find another way. Her defiance might have cost her dearly in that moment, but the fire of her determination had not been extinguished. It merely smoldered, waiting for the

CHAPTER 5

opportune moment to erupt once more.

Chapter 6

The throbbing agony in Anya's ribs persisted, each breath a shallow, guarded inhale. Days blurred into a painful monotony within the confines of her restraints. The Network personnel checked on her periodically, their expressions clinical, offering nutrient paste that tasted like ash. Silas did not reappear.

As her body slowly began the arduous process of healing, Anya focused inward, seeking solace in the familiar hum of the Spire device. It rested, inert, in a shielded compartment across the room, a constant reminder of the power she couldn't access. Yet, even in its dormant state, she felt a faint connection, a subtle thrumming beneath the surface of her skin.

One night, as a wave of particularly sharp pain radiated through her torso, a strange sensation accompanied it. It began as a faint warmth, centered around her injured ribs, a gentle pulse that resonated with the distant hum of the Spire device. It was unlike the usual surge of power she felt when actively using it; this was softer, more internal.

The warmth intensified, spreading through her chest, a soothing balm against the raw agony. Anya frowned, focusing her senses. It felt... alive, as if the device itself was responding to her pain, emitting a subtle energy that was somehow... mending.

As the hours passed, the throbbing in her ribs lessened. The sharp, stabbing pain with each breath dulled to a manageable ache. Anya remained still, her mind racing. Could the Spire device possess healing properties she hadn't been aware of? Was this an automatic response to her injury, a subconscious function of their symbiotic link?

By the next morning, the difference was undeniable. While tenderness remained, the debilitating pain had receded significantly. She could take deeper breaths without the searing agony that had plagued her for days. The broken ribs, though still damaged, felt as if they had begun to knit themselves back together at an accelerated rate.

The Network personnel who came to check on her noted her improved condition with detached interest, attributing it to her "resilient physiology." But Anya knew better. This wasn't just her body healing; it was the subtle, almost imperceptible influence of the Spire device, a silent, internal mending she hadn't consciously controlled.

A new understanding of her connection to the artifact began to dawn. It wasn't just a source of power; it was intrinsically linked to her well-being, perhaps even possessing a form of self-preservation that extended to her own physical form.

The realization sparked a flicker of renewed hope within the confines of her captivity. If the device could heal her, what other untapped potential lay dormant within their bond? And more importantly, if it was so intrinsically linked to her, could the Network truly sever that connection without risking irreparable harm to her?

As she lay there, the faint hum of the Spire device a silent companion, Anya knew one thing for certain. Her connection to this ancient technology was far deeper and more mysterious than even she had imagined. And perhaps, just perhaps, it held the key not only to her own survival but also to the liberation of her family and the downfall of the Network. The whispers within her were growing stronger, hinting at possibilities she had yet to explore.

Chapter 7

The localized blackout plunged Sector Gamma into chaos. Alarms blared erratically, emergency lights flickered, and the hum of the Network's machinery stuttered and died in patches. It was Jax's handiwork, a digital ghost wreaking havoc on their systems.

Whisper, cloaked in shadow-dampening fabric and moving with a practiced silence, led Boris and two other trusted members of their syndicate – a nimble tech expert named Kai and a formidable close-quarters fighter known only as "Rook" – through the darkened corridors. Their intel, gleaned from Anya's brief energy signature and Jax's infiltration of the facility's architectural schematics, had led them to the research labs deep within this sector.

"Anya's signal was strongest in Sub-Level Four, Lab Seven," Whisper hissed into her comm, her cybernetic eyes cutting through the gloom. "Boris, you and Rook take point. Kai, stick with me, we'll disable any internal security measures we encounter."

The facility was in lockdown, but the blackout had sown confusion among the Network personnel. They moved cautiously, using the flickering emergency lights and the chaos as cover. They bypassed laser grids and pressure sensors, Kai's nimble fingers working magic on access panels.

They reached Sub-Level Four, the air growing colder, the hum of more advanced technology subtly vibrating through the floor. Lab Seven's door was reinforced steel, sealed tight.

"Stand back," Boris grunted, hefting a compact energy cutter. The beam sliced through the metal with a shower of sparks, and the heavy door swung inward with a groan.

Inside, the lab was dimly lit by emergency strobes. Anya was strapped to a medical bed, her eyes snapping open as they entered. Relief flooded her face, quickly followed by a look of desperate urgency.

"Whisper! You came!"

"We always come for our own, Anya," Whisper replied, moving quickly to release her restraints.

"Mother! She's in the next room!" Anya exclaimed, gesturing towards another sealed door within the lab.

While Boris and Rook secured the area, Whisper and Kai worked to override the second door's lock. It slid open to reveal a smaller examination room. Elena lay on a similar medical bed, her eyes wide with fear and confusion.

"Mother!" Anya rushed to her side, embracing her tightly.

"Anya... you're here..." Elena whispered, her voice trembling.

"We're getting you out," Whisper said, her gaze sweeping the room. "Where's Misha?"

A shadow fell over Elena's face. "He... they took him somewhere else. Deeper. He wasn't here."

A cold dread gripped Anya's heart. They had rescued her and her mother, a small victory hard-won. But Misha was still in the Network's clutches, further into their nightmarish facility.

Sirens wailed in the distance, growing closer. "We're out of time," Boris growled. "The blackout won't last forever."

CHAPTER 7

"We have to go," Whisper said, her hand on Anya's arm. "We'll find him, Anya. I promise. But we need to get you and your mother to safety first."

Torn between relief and a gnawing fear for Misha, Anya nodded reluctantly. They had achieved the impossible, breaking into the Network's stronghold. But their mission was far from over. As they moved swiftly back through the darkened corridors, leaving the chaotic remnants of their intrusion behind, the unspoken promise hung in the air: they would return for Misha. They had to.

Chapter 8

The escape from Chrysalis Mark II was a blur of adrenaline and whispered commands. Boris's modified transport, a hulking shadow against the flickering city lights, tore through the pre-dawn streets, weaving through deserted industrial zones and forgotten underpasses. Elena, still weak and disoriented, leaned heavily on Anya, her hand clutching her daughter's arm with a desperate grip.

But the Network's response was swift and brutal. Within hours, Anya and her mother were once again the most wanted fugitives in Veridia. Their faces, alongside Whisper's and the blurred images of Boris, Jax, and Kai, plastered every public screen and Network terminal. The bounty on their heads had doubled.

Anya knew they couldn't stay in one place for long. The Network's surveillance was omnipresent, their reach seemingly limitless. They needed to disappear, to become ghosts in the machine once more.

Leaving Elena in the relative safety of a hidden safe house – a network of interconnected abandoned apartments managed by sympathetic Undercity dwellers – Anya and Whisper struck out into the labyrinthine depths of Veridia. This time, however, Anya was different. The weeks of captivity, the forced demonstrations of her abilities, the horrifying glimpse into Project Chimera, and the desperate rescue had forged a new layer of steel within her.

She moved with a heightened awareness, her senses sharpened by the constant threat. She utilized the city's underbelly with a practiced ease, navigating the crowded markets and shadowed alleyways, blending seamlessly with the flow of the downtrodden and the forgotten. She anticipated Network patrols, recognizing their patterns and exploiting their blind spots.

When a pair of Enforcers, their faces grim and their energy weapons charged, spotted her near a black market tech exchange, Anya didn't hesitate. She used the dense crowd as cover, her movements fluid and unpredictable. A well-placed tripwire fashioned from discarded synth-cable sent one sprawling, while she vaulted over a stack of discarded hover-drives, disappearing into the maze of stalls before the other Enforcer could react.

Whisper, a shadow at her side, provided crucial intel, her network feeding them real-time updates on Network movements. "They've deployed enhanced surveillance drones in Sector Seven, Anya. Avoid the elevated walkways."

Anya adapted instantly, leading them through the grimy service tunnels beneath the sector, the air thick with the smell of ozone and decay. Her knowledge of the city's forgotten infrastructure, once a means of mere survival, was now a vital weapon in their evasion.

The Network tried to anticipate her movements, deploying tracking teams based on her previous patterns. But Anya had learned from her mistakes. She varied her routes, utilized dead drops for communication, and employed layers of digital camouflage to mask her presence on the network. Jax, though still under Whisper's watchful eye, proved invaluable in creating these digital diversions, his skills turning the Network's own surveillance against them.

Anya's connection to the Spire device remained a closely guarded secret. She used its subtle enhancements sparingly, relying more on her honed reflexes and street smarts. She knew that any significant energy surge could potentially alert the Network, especially now that they had a better understanding of its signature.

Hunted once again, Anya was no longer just running. She was evading, adapting, and learning. The Network might have thought they had broken her, but they had only tempered her resolve. The ghost in the machine had returned, more elusive and more dangerous than ever before, her every move a testament to her growth and her unwavering determination to rescue Misha and dismantle the Network's monstrous plans.

Chapter 9

Days bled into a tense, precarious existence. Anya and Whisper moved like phantoms through Veridia's underbelly, their every step shadowed by the Network's relentless pursuit. Elena remained safe, but the weight of Misha's continued captivity pressed heavily on Anya, a constant ache in her chest that no amount of evasion could dull.

The successful rescue had emboldened their small syndicate. Others, witnessing their defiance splashed across the public screens, began to reach out through encrypted channels, offering assistance, sharing information, their own stories of Network oppression and loss. The seeds of rebellion, sown in the chaos of their actions, were beginning to sprout.

Whisper, ever the pragmatist, was cautiously optimistic. "We're gaining traction, Anya. People are seeing the Network's true face, their ruthlessness. But these are just whispers in the dark. We need more, something to truly galvanize the city."

Anya, her gaze distant as she cleaned a scavenged energy pistol, nodded slowly. "Misha is that something. He's a symbol now, proof of their cruelty. But we can't risk another direct assault, not yet. They'll be expecting it."

Their current sanctuary was a sprawling network of abandoned train tunnels beneath the city's central district, a labyrinthine space that offered both concealment and multiple escape routes. It was here, amidst the echoing silence and the rustle of unseen creatures, that they held their clandestine meetings, the faces of new recruits illuminated by the flickering glow of makeshift lamps.

Jax, still working to atone for his past lapse, had become invaluable in navigating the Network's digital web, feeding them crucial intel and creating sophisticated decoys to divert their attention. Boris, his loyalty unwavering, trained the new recruits in combat and provided them with the rudimentary weaponry they could scavenge or fabricate. Rook, silent and deadly, became their primary scout, her ability to move undetected through the city's shadows unmatched.

But the absence of Misha cast a pall over their growing efforts. Anya found herself constantly replaying the image of the blue glow on his neck, the vacant look in his eyes. The thought of him being subjected to the Network's horrifying experiments fueled a desperate urgency within her.

"Silas showed me what they're doing," Anya said one night, her voice low and filled with a raw anger as she recounted the grotesque figures in the Chrysalis lab. "He said Misha was... receptive to their bonding."

A collective shudder ran through the small group gathered around the makeshift table. The implications were terrifying. They weren't just holding Misha; they were actively trying to integrate him into their nightmarish vision.

"We need to understand what that device is, on his neck," Whisper said, her cybernetic eyes focused intently on a grainy schematic Jax had managed to extract. "It's emitting a similar energy signature to the Spire device, but... different. More controlled, more... invasive."

CHAPTER 9

Anya's hand instinctively went to her pouch, where the Spire device pulsed with its familiar warmth. The connection felt different now, tinged with a protective instinct, a silent warning.

"If they can control Misha like that..." Anya began, her voice tight with fear.

"Then we need to find a way to disrupt that control," Whisper finished, her gaze resolute. "We need to understand their technology, find its weaknesses. And we need to find allies within the Network, those who still have a shred of humanity left."

The weight of Misha's absence fueled their rebellion, transforming their desperate flight into a focused resistance. The seeds they had sown were beginning to take root, but the shadow of the Network, and the terrifying fate that awaited Anya's brother, loomed large, a constant reminder of the perilous path they had chosen. The fight for Veridia, and for Anya's family, was far from over. It was only just beginning to truly take shape.

Chapter 10

The flickering holographic message shimmered in the dim tunnel, projected by a device one of their new recruits had nervously handed Whisper. It bore the sigil of the Crimson Hand, a notorious faction that had long opposed the Network's iron grip on Veridia. Their methods, however, were as brutal as their enemy's, their reputation stained with violence and a ruthless disregard for innocent lives.

"They... they say they can help," the recruit stammered, his eyes darting nervously around the tunnel. "They know about Misha. They've been... watching."

Whisper exchanged a wary glance with Anya. The Crimson Hand was a wild card, a force of chaos in a city already teetering on the edge. Their opposition to the Network was undeniable, but their motives were often self-serving, their vision for Veridia a brutal alternative to the Network's sterile control.

Anya felt a surge of desperate hope mixed with a deep unease. The Crimson Hand had resources, information, manpower. They could potentially provide the leverage they desperately needed to rescue Misha. But the cost... the thought of aligning themselves with such a ruthless group sent a shiver down her spine.

A clandestine meeting was arranged in a neutral territory –

the skeletal remains of a pre-Network skyscraper in the lawless Outer Sectors. The Hand's representative was a woman known as Seraphina, her face scarred, her eyes sharp and calculating. She moved with a predatory grace, flanked by heavily armed enforcers whose cybernetic enhancements gleamed ominously in the dim light.

"Petrova," Seraphina's voice was gravelly, devoid of warmth. "You've made quite a stir. The Network is... agitated." A cruel smile touched her lips. "We appreciate a bit of disruption."

"We need your help," Anya stated, cutting to the chase. "My brother... the Network has him. They're experimenting on him."

Seraphina's gaze sharpened. "The Chimera project. Yes, we've been... monitoring their progress. Your brother is of particular interest."

"You know where he is?" Anya pressed, her hope surging.

"We have our sources," Seraphina replied cryptically. "And we have our own reasons for wanting to disrupt their little... unification project." Her eyes flickered to Anya's pouch, where the faint pulse of the Spire device was almost palpable. "Your... unique asset... is also of interest to us."

"What do you want?" Whisper interjected, her voice wary.

"An alliance of convenience," Seraphina said, her smile widening. "We provide you with information, resources, access. In return, you lend us your... talents. We have our own objectives within the Network's infrastructure. Objectives that require a certain... finesse." Her gaze lingered on Anya.

The implications were clear. The Crimson Hand wanted Anya's abilities, her connection to the Spire device, for their own brutal purposes. Their methods, Anya knew, would likely involve bloodshed and a complete disregard for innocent lives.

The moral dilemma weighed heavily on Anya. Aligning with

the Crimson Hand could offer a faster, more direct route to rescuing Misha. Their resources and intelligence were undeniable. But could she stomach their methods? Could she justify potentially sacrificing innocent lives in the name of saving her brother? Was it better to remain a small, principled resistance, even if it meant a longer, more perilous path, or to embrace the darkness in the hope of achieving a greater good – or at least, a personal one? The enemy of her enemy was offering an alliance, but the price of that alliance might be her very soul. The weight of the decision pressed down on her, a chilling question mark hanging over their desperate fight.

Chapter 11

"Absolutely not," Anya said, the words sharper than a shard of synth-glass. "You want us to... finesse things? Your 'finesse' looks a lot like blowing things up and asking questions later." She gestured to Seraphina's heavily armed entourage. "We're trying to save people, not add to the body count."

Seraphina raised a scarred eyebrow, a hint of amusement flickering in her sharp eyes. "Sentimental. I suppose that's why you're in this mess in the first place. Look around, Petrova. This isn't a tea party. The Network doesn't respond to polite requests. Sometimes, you need a bigger hammer." She hefted a wicked-looking energy blade. "We are that hammer."

"A very indiscriminate hammer," Whisper interjected, her voice coolly analytical. "Your methods tend to... collateral damage."

"Collateral is a cost of doing business," Seraphina shrugged. "Besides, the Network's 'innocents' are usually just cogs in their machine. Grease the wheels, the whole thing slows down."

Anya crossed her arms, her resolve firm. "We'll find our own way."

Seraphina leaned forward, her gaze intense. "And how's that going so far? Your brother is still their lab rat, isn't he? Your little band of rebels is growing, commendable, but hardly a match for the Network's legions. We offer you a chance to actually *do* something, Petrova. Real change. Real rescue."

The weight of Misha's captivity settled heavily on Anya again. Seraphina's words, though harsh, held a bitter truth. Their small group was struggling against an overwhelming force. The Crimson Hand, for all their brutality, had the muscle and the network to potentially make a significant impact.

"And what exactly would this 'finesse' entail?" Anya asked, her voice grudging.

Seraphina's lips curved into a predatory smile. "There's a secure data vault in the Network's central archive. Holds sensitive information, the kind that would make even Silas sweat. Retrieving it would cause... significant disruption. A scalpel, not a hammer, for this particular task. Your... unique talents... would be invaluable in bypassing certain security measures." Her gaze flickered pointedly at Anya's pouch.

Anya hesitated. Using the Spire device for the Crimson Hand's objectives felt wrong, a betrayal of its potential. But the image of Misha, with that unsettling blue glow on his neck, flashed in her mind.

Whisper, sensing Anya's internal struggle, spoke softly. "We could use their resources to locate Misha. Information they have access to..."

Anya sighed, the fight draining out of her. The moral high ground felt awfully lonely when her brother's life was on the line. "Fine," she said, the word tasting like defeat. "But no innocents. If your 'finesse' involves hurting anyone who isn't actively working for the Network, the deal's off."

Seraphina chuckled, a dry, rasping sound. "Such idealism. It's almost... endearing. We have our targets, Petrova. You have yours. Let's just say our Venn diagram overlaps where the Network is concerned." She extended a hand, her grip surprisingly firm. "Welcome to the messy side of the revolution."

Anya reluctantly took her hand, the contact feeling cold and transactional. She had just made a deal with the devil, hoping to rescue her angel. The path ahead was fraught with moral peril, but the image of Misha's vacant eyes was a stark reminder of the price of inaction. Sometimes, even the most principled had to get their hands dirty.

Chapter 12

The uneasy truce with the Crimson Hand had opened doors, albeit shadowed ones. Their network, though ruthless, provided Anya with access to fragmented Network archives, information Seraphina offered with a calculating glint in her eye. As they planned their assault on the Zenith Spire to rescue Misha, a gnawing feeling persisted within Anya. The Network's intense interest in her family's "unique affinities," coupled with the familiar blue glow of Misha's implant, hinted at a deeper connection than mere coincidence.

Driven by this unease, Anya began to probe her fragmented memories of her parents, seeking answers in the carefully constructed silence of her past. She recalled hushed conversations, her mother's watchful gaze, a sense of them always living on the edge of something unseen.

Using the Crimson Hand's illicit access to Network databases, Anya sifted through old files, birth records, and property deeds. Most were sterile, scrubbed clean of anything significant. Then, she found a heavily redacted file bearing her mother's maiden name: Vanya Rostova. Within the scrambled text, certain keywords snagged her attention: "Project Chimera – early research," "neural sensitivity," "protective measures," and, intriguingly, a codename: "Seer."

CHAPTER 12

The term "protective measures" resonated with Anya's faint memories of a life lived with a subtle layer of shielding, a sense of her parents guarding a secret. But from whom? And why the codename?

Driven by this flicker of a lead, Anya sought out the oldest contacts within the Crimson Hand's network, individuals who had been operating in Veridia long before Silas's ascent. In a dimly lit information den in the Outer Sectors, she met a wizened data broker known as "Echo," his eyes sharp despite his age.

"Rostova," the old man rasped, his voice a low hum. "Yes... your mother. They called her Seer, back in the day. She was... sensitive. They were interested in her, even back then, in the early days of Chimera's development."

Fragmented images flickered at the edge of Anya's awareness: her mother, younger but with the same determined set to her jaw, undergoing what looked like neurological scans. Shadowy figures in Network uniforms, hushed and intense discussions.

"Interested in what? Her... sensitivity? The codename?" Anya pressed.

The old man nodded slowly. "To the old tech. The Spires... they resonate with certain individuals. Your mother... she had a natural affinity, a stronger connection than most. And the codename... it referred to her ability to... perceive things others couldn't. Subtle energy flows, future probabilities... whispers of the Spires themselves."

A faint memory surfaced: her mother's hand gently guiding Anya's towards a cool, smooth surface that hummed with a barely perceptible energy. A whispered warning: "Be careful, Anya. Some knowledge... attracts unwanted attention."

The pieces began to click into place. Her own connection to the Spire device wasn't random. Her mother had possessed a similar, perhaps even more potent, sensitivity, something the Network had been aware of even before Anya was born. The codename "Seer" painted a picture of abilities far beyond mere resonance. Misha's implant, pulsing with that familiar energy, was likely a twisted attempt to exploit that same inherent, precognitive connection. Her family wasn't just victims; they were targets by design, their bloodline holding a key to the Network's ambitions.

The old data broker offered one final, cryptic piece of information. "There were whispers... back then. About families with a... resonance, with the Seer bloodline. Some tried to hide, to sever the connection. Others... sought to understand it, to control it."

Anya's mind raced. Had her parents been trying to protect her from the Network's interest in their Seer lineage? Had they known about the Spire device and its potential link to their abilities? The weight of her family's hidden history settled upon her, a new layer of complexity added to their desperate fight. Misha wasn't just a prisoner; he was a link to a past Anya was only beginning to grasp, a past that held both danger and perhaps, the key to unlocking the full potential of her own inherited power.

Chapter 13

The power struggle for Veridia was a brutal, three-pronged conflict. The Network, under Silas's increasingly obsessive control, tightened its grip, Project Chimera's monstrous forms multiplying in their hidden labs. The Crimson Hand, led by the ruthless Seraphina, carved out territories in the fringes, their chaotic violence a constant thorn in the Network's side. And Anya's group, smaller but driven by a fierce moral core and a desperate love for family, navigated the treacherous landscape between these two behemoths.

The uneasy alliance with the Crimson Hand was a necessary evil, their resources and intel on the Zenith Spire offering the only viable path to rescuing Misha. But the tension was palpable. Seraphina's pragmatic brutality clashed with Anya's unwavering principles, their shared goal overshadowed by fundamentally different ideologies.

As Anya and Whisper finalized their infiltration plan with Seraphina and her lieutenants in a Crimson Hand stronghold – a heavily fortified, repurposed factory in the Industrial Zone – the air crackled with distrust. The Hand's enforcers, their cybernetic enhancements gleaming under harsh fluorescent lights, regarded Anya's team with open suspicion.

"The data vault retrieval remains paramount," Seraphina

reiterated, her gaze sharp. "The information within will cripple Network operations for weeks. Your... unique talents... are essential for bypassing its security. Your Seer bloodline might even perceive weaknesses in their digital fortress."

Anya met her gaze, her own unwavering. "Misha comes first. The data vault is a secondary objective. And I reiterate: no innocent blood spilled for your goals. Our alliance is contingent on that." The revelation of her mother's codename and abilities added a new layer to her resolve. She wouldn't let her inherited power be used for the Crimson Hand's violent ends.

Seraphina offered a cynical smile. "Innocence is a luxury in Veridia, Petrova. But we understand your... reservations. For now, our targets align. The Network pays for what they've done."

Whisper, ever vigilant, scanned their surroundings, her cybernetic eyes picking up subtle shifts in the Crimson Hand enforcers' postures. "Their priorities are clear, Anya. They see us as a means to an end."

"We see them as a means to Misha," Anya replied, her voice low but firm. "It's a dangerous game, but it's the only one we have right now." The knowledge of her mother's Seer abilities gave her a chilling insight into the potential dangers ahead, and the value the Network placed on her family's bloodline.

The three factions stood in a precarious balance. The Network, confident in its technological superiority, underestimated the volatile forces gathering in the shadows and the latent power within Anya. The Crimson Hand, driven by a brutal ambition for control, saw Anya's unique abilities as a weapon to be wielded. And Anya's group, fueled by love and a growing understanding of their heritage, prepared to walk a dangerous tightrope, their actions potentially igniting a city-wide conflict that could either liberate Veridia or plunge it into further chaos. The rescue of Misha was the immediate goal, but the fight for the city's future had become a complex dance between three distinct powers, each with their own agenda and their own definition of victory, now colored by the secrets of the Seer bloodline.

Chapter 14

The infiltration of the Zenith Spire was a tense ballet of shadows and silenced alarms. Anya, guided by the Crimson Hand's rudimentary schematics and her own heightened senses, moved alongside Whisper, Boris, and a small contingent of Seraphina's most skilled operatives. The uneasy alliance held, for now, their shared goal of disrupting the Network overriding their inherent distrust.

The data vault was located deep within the Spire's secure levels, a fortress of encrypted systems and lethal countermeasures. Seraphina's team focused on the physical security, their brutal efficiency carving a path through Network enforcers. Anya, however, was the key to bypassing the digital defenses.

Using her innate connection to the ancient technology, a resonance amplified by the Spire device, she could perceive the subtle flows of energy within the Network's systems, the invisible pathways of data. It was a crude, intuitive form of interface, but it allowed her to sense vulnerabilities that conventional hacking couldn't detect.

As they reached the vault's heavily shielded door, Jax, operating remotely from their hidden base, fed Anya fragmented access codes gleaned from his perilous forays into the Network's network. But the final layer of security remained impenetrable, a complex energy field that defied conventional decryption.

"This is it," Seraphina growled, her energy blade humming. "Stand back."

But Anya held up a hand. Focusing her will, she reached out with her senses, feeling the intricate dance of energy within the shield. It pulsed with a familiar rhythm, a distorted echo of the Spire device's own signature. A chilling realization dawned within her. The Network wasn't just trying to replicate the technology; they were actively integrating it into their core systems.

Closing her eyes, Anya channeled the energy of her device, letting it resonate with the field. It was a dangerous gamble, a direct interaction that could trigger alarms or even a lethal feedback loop. But as the two energies intertwined, a subtle pathway shimmered into existence within the shield.

"Now!" Anya hissed, stepping through the momentary gap before it sealed shut.

Inside the vault, the air hummed with the power of countless data servers. Anya moved quickly, guided by Jax's fragmented map. The primary data core was a monolithic structure in the center of the room, its surface covered in blinking lights and intricate interfaces.

While Seraphina's team secured the perimeter, Anya connected a neural interface cable Jax had provided to the core. Lines of encrypted data scrolled across her vision, a chaotic torrent of information. It was overwhelming, but she focused, searching for specific keywords: "Chimera," "Rostova," "Subject M."

Then she found it – a heavily encrypted sub-directory labeled "Project Nightingale." As Jax's decryption algorithms slowly peeled back the layers of code, a series of chilling files began to emerge.

Schematics detailed advanced neural integration technology far beyond the grotesque hybrids Anya had witnessed. These designs were elegant, precise, hinting at a complete merging of consciousness.

Then came the files on her family. Detailed analyses of Elena's unique neural architecture, confirming her Seer lineage and its amplified sensitivity to the ancient technology. But it was Misha's file that sent a shard of ice through Anya's heart.

Diagrams illustrated the implant on his neck, revealing it to be a highly advanced neural control device, capable of not just facilitating integration but of completely overriding his will. His "receptivity" wasn't natural; it was forced.

Finally, Anya found a log file, the last entry chillingly recent. It detailed a new phase of Project Chimera, a city-wide integration initiative codenamed "Resonance Cascade." The Network planned to use the amplified energy of the Zenith Spire, coupled with their understanding of the Seer bloodline and their control technology, to broadcast a neural resonance across Veridia, subtly influencing the minds of the populace, conditioning them for eventual full integration. Misha, with his implant, was to be the initial amplification node.

The vault held another, even more terrifying secret. A physical device, humming softly on a pedestal in a secure alcove. It was small, intricate, and pulsed with a faint, familiar blue light – a miniature Spire device, far more refined and powerful than the one Anya possessed. The file identified it as a "Resonance Amplifier," the key to the city-wide integration.

The discovery was staggering, horrifying. The Network's plans were far grander and more insidious than Anya had imagined. They weren't just creating monsters; they were planning to enslave an entire city. And Misha was at the center of their terrifying scheme.

As Anya stared at the Resonance Amplifier, a silent alarm blared in the back of her mind. A subtle shift in the vault's energy field, a flicker in the corner of her vision. They had been compromised.

"We've been made!" Whisper's voice crackled in her ear. "Get out now!"

Anya grabbed the data drive containing the Project Nightingale files, her mind reeling from the weight of her discovery. The vault held the key to understanding the Network's ultimate goal and the horrifying fate of her family. But in uncovering these secrets, she had walked directly into the heart of the beast, and the beast was now wide awake. The danger had just escalated exponentially.

Chapter 15

The escape from the Zenith Spire was a desperate scramble against overwhelming odds. Network security forces, alerted to the breach, converged on their location with lethal efficiency. Seraphina's brutal tactics, while effective initially, now painted them as glaring targets in the Spire's sterile corridors.

Boris and Rook provided a fierce rearguard, their heavy weaponry tearing through the pursuing Enforcers, buying Anya and Whisper precious seconds to evacuate with the stolen data drive. Jax, his voice strained, guided them remotely through the Spire's ventilation shafts, the narrow confines a claustrophobic contrast to the vast, echoing chambers they had just breached.

Anya, clutching the data drive containing the horrifying truth of Project Nightingale, felt the weight of the city's fate resting on her shoulders. Whisper moved beside her, her cybernetic eyes scanning for threats even as they navigated the tight spaces.

Their extraction point was a high-speed transport dock on the Spire's outer hull, a risky gambit relying on the Crimson Hand's pre-planted escape vehicle. As they burst onto the platform, bathed in the cold glare of the city lights, the sleek transport shimmered into view.

But the Network had anticipated their move. A squadron of heavily armed interceptors descended from the sky, their energy cannons blazing. The platform erupted in a chaotic firefight.

Boris roared, unleashing a barrage of plasma fire, taking down one of the interceptors in a fiery explosion. Rook moved with a silent, deadly grace, disabling security drones with precise energy pulses. Seraphina and her remaining operatives fought with a ferocity born of desperation.

Anya, though not a frontline fighter, used her agility and the Spire device's subtle enhancements to evade enemy fire, her focus on reaching the transport. Whisper, her cybernetic eyes tracking multiple threats, provided covering fire while simultaneously guiding Anya.

Just as Anya was about to board the transport, a searing energy blast ripped through the platform, striking Rook. He staggered, a smoking hole in his chest, before collapsing silently onto the metal grating.

Anya cried out, her heart clenching. Rook, the silent protector, gone in an instant.

The remaining interceptors intensified their attack. The Crimson Hand's transport shuddered under the barrage. "We have to go!" Seraphina yelled, shoving Anya inside.

As the transport's engines roared to life, lifting them precariously from the ravaged platform, another energy blast slammed into their rear. The vehicle lurched violently, throwing its occupants against the bulkhead.

Whisper cried out, clutching her side. A crimson stain bloomed on her jacket.

"Whisper!" Anya scrambled to her friend's side, her heart pounding with terror. The energy blast had ripped through the transport's armor, tearing into Whisper's flesh.

"Go... get the data..." Whisper gasped, her face pale with pain, her breath coming in ragged gasps.

Anya's mind reeled. Rook dead, Whisper gravely injured. The raid had been successful, the data acquired. But the cost... the cost was devastating.

Boris, his face grim, piloted the damaged transport through the chaotic airspace, dodging pursuing Network craft. Seraphina, her usual bravado replaced by a hard-edged fury, barked orders at her remaining operatives, assessing the damage.

Anya cradled Whisper in her arms, the crimson stain spreading, her pleas for her friend to hold on met with weak, pain-filled moans. The weight of their losses, the brutal price of their defiance, crashed down on Anya. The information they had risked everything to obtain was crucial, but the victory felt hollow, stained with the blood of their fallen comrade and the agonizing reality of Whisper's fading strength. The fight against the Network had just become even more personal, fueled by grief and a burning desire for retribution.

Chapter 16

The damaged transport limped towards their hidden safe house, the silence within broken only by Whisper's shallow, ragged breaths and Anya's frantic attempts to staunch the bleeding. The crimson stain on Whisper's jacket continued to spread, a horrifying testament to the Network's brutal retaliation.

As Anya pressed a makeshift bandage against Whisper's wound, her mind raced, replaying the events of the Zenith Spire raid. It had been too easy, in some ways. They had acquired the data, but the Network's response had been immediate, targeted, almost as if they had known exactly where to intercept them.

A cold suspicion began to snake through Anya's fear and grief. How had the Network reacted so swiftly? How had they known their extraction point with such precision? The thought was a venomous whisper in the chaos of her emotions: betrayal.

Back at the safe house, a tense quiet descended. Boris, his face grim, secured the perimeter. Jax, his usual nervous energy replaced by a haunted stillness, worked to stabilize Whisper with the limited medical supplies they possessed. Seraphina and her remaining Crimson Hand operatives stood apart, their expressions unreadable, the cost of the raid evident in their reduced numbers.

As Whisper drifted in and out of consciousness, her grip on

Anya's hand weakening, Anya's gaze swept across the faces of her allies. Boris, loyal and steadfast. Jax, whose past betrayal still cast a long shadow. The new recruits, their allegiances still untested. And the remaining members of the Crimson Hand, their motives forever suspect.

The data drive lay on a nearby table, the key to understanding the Network's horrifying plans. But the victory felt hollow, poisoned by the suspicion that someone among them had tipped off the Network.

The realization hit Anya with the force of a physical blow. Weeks ago, when she had first sought information about the Spire device, she had confided in Jax. He had logged her query, a seemingly innocuous act. But the timing of the Network's intensified search, the precision of their initial attack... it mirrored the events of the Zenith Spire raid too closely.

Her gaze locked onto Jax, who was now hunched over Whisper, his brow furrowed in apparent concern. A cold fury began to simmer beneath Anya's grief. Had he been compromised again? Had the Network, or perhaps even the Crimson Hand with their own hidden agendas, turned him?

Anya's voice, low and dangerous, cut through the silence. "Jax."

He looked up, his eyes wide with a feigned innocence. "Anya? How's Whisper?"

"She's dying," Anya said, her gaze unwavering. "And I want to know how the Network knew where to find us at the Zenith Spire. It was too precise. Someone told them."

The air in the room thickened. All eyes turned to Jax, whose face paled visibly. He stammered, "I... I don't know what you mean, Anya. I was working remotely, trying to help you get in and out."

"You were also the one who knew about the extraction point," Anya pressed, her voice hardening. "You integrated the Crimson Hand's flight plan into our exit strategy."

Seraphina's sharp eyes narrowed, her hand instinctively moving towards the energy blade at her hip. "What are you implying, Petrova?"

"I'm saying we have a traitor in our midst," Anya said, her gaze still locked on Jax. "Someone who led the Network right to us. Someone who might have been playing us all along."

Whisper coughed weakly, her eyes fluttering open. She looked at Anya, a flicker of understanding in her pain-filled gaze. "Anya... the logs... months ago..." Her voice was barely a whisper.

The pieces clicked into place for Anya, Whisper's dying words confirming her terrible suspicion. Jax. He had been the point of contact, the seemingly harmless tech expert. But his past actions, coupled with the uncanny accuracy of the Network's attacks, painted a damning picture.

Trust, the fragile foundation of their rebellion, shattered into a million pieces. Anya looked at the faces around her, her heart heavy with betrayal and a chilling sense of isolation. With Whisper fading, and the horrifying truth of Project Nightingale now in their hands, Anya realized she was surrounded by shadows, unsure of who she could truly trust. The enemy wasn't just the Network; it was within their own ranks, a serpent they had unknowingly welcomed into their fold. The cost of their raid was far greater than just the lives lost; it was the erosion of the very bonds that held them together.

Chapter 17

Whisper's shallow breaths filled the tense silence of the safe house, each gasp a painful reminder of their devastating loss. Anya, her face set in a grim mask, watched Jax as Seraphina's enforcers, their expressions cold and unreadable, dragged him towards a makeshift holding cell.

"You're making a mistake, Anya!" Jax protested, his voice laced with a desperate plea. "I swear, I didn't betray you! I wouldn't betray Whisper!"

Anya's gaze hardened. "The logs don't lie, Jax. And Whisper... she remembered. Months ago. You led them to us, then and at the Zenith Spire. Whether you did it knowingly or not, you're responsible for what happened to Rook. For what's happening to Whisper."

Seraphina watched the exchange with a calculating gaze. "Sentimentality is a luxury we can't afford, Petrova. But your... suspicion... is understandable. We'll keep him contained. For now."

With Jax secured, the focus shifted to Whisper. Her condition was deteriorating rapidly, the energy weapon blast having inflicted severe internal damage. Their limited medical supplies were woefully inadequate.

Anya knelt beside Whisper, her heart heavy with grief and a

CHAPTER 17

growing sense of desperation. "Hold on, Whisper. Please. We'll get you help."

Whisper's eyes flickered open, her gaze weak but resolute. "Anya... listen... you have to... be strong... for Misha..."

Her voice trailed off, her breathing becoming more labored. Anya felt a surge of helplessness, a desperate need to do something, anything, to save her friend.

Seraphina stepped forward, her scarred face unreadable. "There's nothing we can do here. The Network has... resources. They could potentially stabilize her, even... repair the damage."

Anya's head snapped up, her eyes wide with a mixture of hope and disbelief. "You mean... take her to the Network?"

Seraphina's lips curved into a cruel smile. "An alliance of convenience, remember? They have what she needs. And in return... you offer them something they desire even more."

Anya's mind raced. Handing Whisper over to the Network felt like a betrayal, a horrifying echo of Misha's captivity. But the alternative... watching her die... was unthinkable.

"What do you want?" Anya asked, her voice tight with a desperate resignation.

"Your... talents," Seraphina replied, her gaze fixed on Anya's pouch. "You will infiltrate another Network facility, a weapons research lab. They're developing a new type of energy weapon, one that could potentially disrupt the Spire device's resonance. We need the schematics. And you... you can get them for us."

Anya stared at Seraphina, her mind reeling. She was being forced to make an impossible choice: sacrifice Whisper to the Network's clutches in exchange for a mission that could potentially save her life, but further their own brutal agenda.

As Whisper's breathing grew even more shallow, Anya felt a cold resolve hardening within her. She would do whatever it took to save her friend, even if it meant embracing the darkness she had so fiercely resisted.

"Fine," Anya said, her voice devoid of emotion. "I'll do it. But if anything happens to Whisper... if they so much as lay a hand on her... this alliance is over. And I will make you pay."

Seraphina nodded slowly, a hint of respect flickering in her eyes. "Understood, Petrova. We have a deal. Now, let's get your friend to the Network. And then... we train you."

Anya looked down at Whisper, her heart heavy with a mixture of grief and a terrifying determination. She had made a pact with the devil, and now, she would learn to fight like one. The serpent's embrace was tightening around her, and she would have to become just as ruthless, just as brutal, to survive and to save those she loved.

Chapter 18

The Network facility Seraphina directed Anya to was a labyrinth of gleaming corridors and heavily guarded research labs, a stark contrast to the gritty underbelly Anya was accustomed to. The promise of Whisper receiving Network-level medical care hung heavy in the air, a fragile lifeline that spurred Anya forward despite the gnawing unease in her gut.

Using her burgeoning, brutal fighting skills – honed in the harsh, unforgiving training sessions with Seraphina's enforcers – Anya moved through the facility with a newfound ruthlessness. She neutralized guards with swift, efficient strikes, her movements devoid of hesitation, the ghost of Rook's silent efficiency guiding her.

The schematics Seraphina provided led her to a heavily fortified research lab, the supposed location of the disruptive energy weapon. But as Anya bypassed the final security door, she found not a weapon, but a data terminal displaying a live feed of Whisper, strapped to a medical bed in a Network intensive care unit. Silas's face filled the adjacent screen, his expression a chilling blend of amusement and triumph.

"Clever girl, Anya," his voice echoed through the lab's speakers. "But sentimentality remains your weakness. The weapon was never real. Your friend, however... she is quite real. And her survival… depends entirely on your continued cooperation."

Rage, cold and sharp, pierced through Anya's fear. It was a trap, a cruel manipulation orchestrated by Silas. Whisper was a pawn, held hostage to ensure Anya's compliance.

As Silas continued his taunts, a secondary alarm blared through the facility. Anya's presence had been detected. She had walked directly into their snare.

A desperate scramble ensued. Anya fought her way back through the facility, Network security forces converging on her position. The brutal efficiency Seraphina had drilled into her kept her alive, but the weight of Silas's betrayal and Whisper's precarious situation fueled a reckless fury.

She managed to reach the extraction point, a maintenance tunnel leading to the outside. But as she burst into the night air, a figure stood silhouetted against the city lights – Seraphina.

"The data?" Seraphina demanded, her hand outstretched.

"It was a trap," Anya snarled, her voice raw with fury. "There was no weapon. They have Whisper!"

Seraphina's expression remained impassive. "A calculated risk. The information Silas revealed… about Whisper's condition… was it accurate?"

Before Anya could answer, a high-pitched whine filled the air. A Network interceptor, faster and more heavily armed than the ones they had faced before, descended rapidly. A searing energy blast struck the ground near Anya, throwing her off her feet.

Seraphina reacted instantly, firing a burst from her energy weapon, forcing the interceptor to veer away. "We need to move!"

They retreated into the shadows, the interceptor circling overhead. Anya's mind was a maelstrom of rage and despair. Silas had played her, used Whisper as bait.

CHAPTER 18

Then, a message crackled through Anya's comm, a scrambled signal she barely recognized. It was Jax, his voice choked with emotion.

"Anya... Whisper... she's gone. They... they couldn't stabilize her. I... I'm so sorry..."

The words hit Anya like a physical blow, stealing her breath, crushing her spirit. Whisper, her steadfast ally, her voice of reason, the one who had believed in her from the start... gone. Because of Silas's cruelty. Because of Anya's desperate gamble.

A raw, primal scream tore from Anya's throat, echoing through the deserted alleyway. Seraphina watched her, her scarred face betraying a flicker of something akin to understanding.

The personal loss was devastating, a gaping wound in Anya's heart. But amidst the grief, a cold, unyielding determination began to solidify. Silas would pay for this. The Network would pay for this. The phantom weapon had cost her everything, and now, fueled by a burning desire for vengeance, Anya Petrova was no longer just fighting for her family or the city. She was fighting for Whisper. And she would not rest until Silas and his monstrous regime were reduced to ashes.

Chapter 19

The air in the Crimson Hand's temporary hideout, a cavernous, dilapidated warehouse filled with scavenged tech and the lingering scent of stale synth-smoke, was thick with a suffocating tension. The triumphant return from the Data Pipe District was overshadowed by the gaping wound Whisper's death had left in Anya's heart.

Boris moved silently, setting down a ration pack in front of Anya, his face a grim mask of sympathy. Other Crimson Hand operatives eyed Anya with a wary respect, having witnessed her cold fury during the drone takedowns. Seraphina stood apart, her arms crossed, observing the aftermath with a calculating detachment.

Anya ignored the food, her gaze fixed on the makeshift medical bay in the corner where Whisper's empty cot stood, a stark reminder of her absence. The grief was a physical weight, pressing down on her, twisting her gut.

Then, the door to Jax's temporary holding cell hissed open. Seraphina, after a brief, whispered conversation with one of her lieutenants, had decided he was needed. His technical skills were too valuable to keep him locked away indefinitely, especially with the Network now fully aware of their movements.

Jax emerged, his shoulders slumped, his eyes red-rimmed

CHAPTER 19

and bloodshot. He scanned the room, his gaze settling on Anya, who was now standing, her fists clenched at her sides.

"Anya... I... I heard about Whisper," Jax began, his voice cracking with genuine remorse. "I'm so sorry. I swear, I didn't mean for any of this to happen. The Network... they had something on me, they threatened my family, I had no choice..."

He took a step towards her, his hand tentatively reaching out. "Please, Anya. I loved Whisper. She was a friend. I never wanted to hurt her."

Anya's vision narrowed, the grief and betrayal consuming her. The image of Whisper, bleeding out in her arms, flashed behind her eyes. Jax's stammered excuses, his desperate pleas for forgiveness, grated on her already raw nerves. He had led them to her. He had facilitated the trap. He was why Whisper was gone.

The raw fury ignited within her, stripping away all logic, all reason.

"You *had* a choice, Jax!" Anya snarled, her voice low and trembling with suppressed rage. "You chose them! You chose to put us all at risk! And now... now Whisper is dead because of you!"

Before Jax could react, before anyone could intervene, Anya moved. It wasn't the fluid grace of her Spire-enhanced movements, nor the brutal efficiency Seraphina had taught her. This was raw, unadulterated anger, channeled into a single, devastating blow.

Her fist connected squarely with Jax's face. The sickening thud echoed through the silent warehouse. Jax cried out, stumbling backward, his hands flying to his rapidly swelling nose. A thin stream of blood began to trickle from his nostril.

He looked at Anya, shock and pain warring in his eyes. "Anya...

what—?"

"That's for Whisper," Anya said, her voice shaking with emotion, her chest heaving. "And if you ever betray us again, if you ever put anyone else in danger, I swear to all the gods of this forgotten city, I will finish what the Network started."

Seraphina, who had watched the entire exchange without moving, offered a dry, almost approving nod. "Understood, Petrova. Message delivered." Her gaze flickered to Jax, who was still clutching his face. "Get him to work. He's more useful at a terminal than bleeding on the floor."

Jax, though clearly hurt, didn't argue. He slowly straightened, his eyes still wide with the shock of Anya's unexpected violence, and retreated to his makeshift workstation.

Anya stood in the center of the warehouse, her knuckles aching, her chest still heaving. The punch had released a fraction of the raw, consuming grief, but it hadn't quelled the pain. Whisper was gone. And the betrayal of Jax, the man she had trusted, had solidified a cold, hard resolve within her.

Chapter 20

The punch to Jax's face had been a visceral release, but it did little to mend the gaping wound in Anya's heart. The grief for Whisper, fueled by the cold fury at Jax's betrayal, transformed into a burning need for control, for strength, for a way to ensure such a loss never happened again. Seraphina, observing Anya's simmering rage, understood.

"Good," Seraphina grunted during their next brutal training session. They were in a disused, heavily reinforced training room within the Crimson Hand's hideout, the air thick with the smell of sweat and ozone. "You're learning to use your anger, Petrova. Don't suppress it. Channel it."

Seraphina moved with a predatory grace, her scarred face a mask of intense concentration. She demonstrated a series of close-quarters combat moves, each designed to exploit an opponent's vulnerabilities, to end a fight swiftly and decisively. This wasn't about flash or acrobatics; it was about brutal efficiency.

"The Network relies on technology, on their implants, on their weapons," Seraphina explained, her voice a low growl as she demonstrated a disarming technique. "They become complacent. Over-reliant. But take away their tech, or make them doubt it, and they're just flesh and bone. Vulnerable."

Anya absorbed every lesson, her mind a sponge, her body a tool she was determined to master. Seraphina forced her to fight without the Spire device, to rely solely on her wits, her reflexes, and the brutal techniques she was being taught. Anya learned to anticipate, to read body language, to exploit subtle shifts in weight and balance. She learned how to use the environment, how to turn a cluttered room into a deadly maze for an opponent.

Her speed increased, her strikes gained a lethal precision. She moved with a newfound fluidity, her movements almost unseen, a ghost in the melee. Without the crutch of the Spire device's amplified senses, Anya's natural instincts sharpened. Her street smarts, honed by years of survival, merged with Seraphina's ruthless combat philosophy, creating a dangerous blend of cunning and raw power.

They sparred for hours, day after day, until Anya's muscles screamed in protest, until exhaustion threatened to drag her down. Seraphina pushed her to her limits, sometimes beyond, seemingly deriving a grim satisfaction from Anya's struggles.

"You're still thinking too much," Seraphina barked after Anya hesitated for a fraction of a second during a disarming drill. "Hesitation is death. When you move, you commit. Make them believe you're already gone before you even strike."

Anya practiced, her mind a relentless loop of movements and counters, until the hesitation vanished, replaced by an almost automatic response. She learned to disarm Network Enforcers in simulations, to slip past their reinforced armor, to target their weak points with devastating effect. She was no longer just fighting; she was becoming a weapon, cold and precise.

One evening, after a particularly grueling session, Seraphina watched Anya execute a complex disarming sequence, her movements fluid and deadly accurate. A rare, almost imperceptible

CHAPTER 20

nod of approval from the Crimson Hand leader.

"You're ready, Petrova," Seraphina stated, her voice gruff. "Ready to make them pay."

Anya looked at her, her eyes hardened by weeks of training and the lingering pain of loss. She had become something new, something dangerous. The Spire device still hummed faintly in her pouch, a potent force she knew she could call upon. But now, she understood that true strength wasn't just about the power within her; it was about the power she could wield without it. The Network had taken so much from her, but they had also forged her into something formidable. The ghost in the machine was learning to fight in the shadows, unseen, unheard, a growing threat without the need for a single energy pulse.

Chapter 21

Silas watched Misha Petrova on the diagnostic screen, a flicker of cold satisfaction in his eyes. The boy was a marvel, a direct conduit to the very essence of the Spires, a living echo of the ancient power. Unlike his sister, Anya, whose bond with the device was a volatile, intuitive connection, Misha's was... malleable. The neural implant, pulsing with its faint blue glow at the base of his neck, ensured that.

"Subject M is exhibiting unprecedented neural receptivity, Director," Dr. Thorne reported, his voice a low hum from a nearby console. "The preliminary resonance induction has been highly successful. His brain activity shows significant synchronization with the Zenith Spire's primary energy signature."

Silas allowed himself a rare, thin smile. The cost of Anya's little raid had been acceptable, a calculated sacrifice. Her desperation had led her to the vault, confirming his suspicions about her lineage and her deeper connection to the Spire technology. Now, with Project Nightingale's full schematics retrieved, and Misha's compliant mind as their primary conduit, the Resonance Cascade was within reach.

"Continue the induction protocol," Silas ordered. "Increase the resonance by three percent. We need to ascertain the maximum sustainable output before full deployment."

CHAPTER 21

On the screen, Misha twitched, a faint tremor running through his young body. His eyes, though open, held a distant, unfocused gaze, reflecting the overwhelming influx of information and energy being channeled through his mind. He was no longer Misha Petrova, the street kid. He was Subject M, a critical component of Project Chimera, a living amplifier for the Network's grand design.

"The Seer lineage is proving even more profound than initial projections suggested," Thorne continued, his voice tinged with scientific awe. "The inherent neural architecture allows for a cleaner, more stable resonance. It's almost as if they were... designed for this purpose."

Silas frowned slightly. "Designed? By whom, Doctor? The ancient ones? A convenient myth to explain what we don't understand." He walked closer to the main display, its intricate diagrams mapping Misha's neural pathways as they interfaced with the Spire's energy. "We simply have the key. And now, we have the lock."

He remembered Anya's defiance, her raw fury during their last encounter. Such wasted potential, such primal, untamed power. But Misha... Misha was controllable. A tool. A means to an end.

The purpose of the current tests was to fully map the resonance pathways within Misha's brain, ensuring that the city-wide neural broadcast would be seamless, undetectable by the general populace until it was too late. The idea was to slowly, subtly, integrate the minds of Veridia's citizens, to condition them for a higher, more unified consciousness under the Network's benevolent control. No more dissent, no more chaos, just perfect order.

Suddenly, a minor fluctuation appeared on the diagnostic

screen – a tiny, almost imperceptible blip in Misha's neural activity, a fleeting moment of resistance. It vanished as quickly as it appeared, swallowed by the overwhelming resonance from the implant.

Thorne glanced at the anomaly, then shrugged. "A minor neural artifact, Director. Perhaps a residual memory attempting to assert itself. It's being suppressed by the primary resonance induction."

Silas's eyes narrowed, a flicker of unease passing through him. Residual memory. Anya's fierce protectiveness for her brother was not easily broken. He had underestimated her once, dismissed her capabilities. He wouldn't make that mistake again. He had taken her most valuable asset, her friend, and left her with nothing but grief and rage. That kind of emotion could be unpredictable.

He turned from the screen, his gaze sweeping across the secure lab. "Maintain constant vigilance. Double the psychic dampeners around this quadrant. I want no outside interference. And prepare for the next phase. The Resonance Cascade will begin within the standard cycle. Veridia awaits its new consciousness."

The anomaly was minor, fleeting, but it stirred a faint whisper of doubt in Silas's mind. A single, defiant echo in the vast, controlled symphony of Misha's resonance. A reminder that even the most perfectly engineered systems could sometimes harbor unforeseen variables. And Anya Petrova, the unpredictable anomaly, was still out there.

Chapter 22

Anya moved through the underbelly of Veridia like a phantom, her senses alive to every shadow, every shift in the air currents. The rage over Whisper's death, the bitter resentment towards Jax, and the burning need for vengeance against Silas had honed her into a living weapon. Seraphina's brutal training had stripped away any lingering hesitation, replacing it with a cold, calculated efficiency. The Spire device, nestled in her pouch, remained dormant, a silent promise of raw power she now understood was a last resort.

The city above hummed with a terrifying normalcy, oblivious to the insidious threat growing within the Network's hidden labs. Anya often found herself staring at the towering skyscrapers, imagining the subtle, almost imperceptible neural resonance Silas intended to broadcast, the invisible chains he planned to weave around the minds of millions. Misha, the amplification node, was at the heart of it.

Her current mission, sanctioned by Seraphina, was to plant a series of advanced signal disruptors near key Network broadcast towers in the Entertainment District. These devices, acquired through the Crimson Hand's less-than-legal channels, were designed to create localized interference, hopefully throwing off the Resonance Cascade when it began. It was a small, desperate measure, a tiny wrench in Silas's grand machinery, but it was *something*.

As she scaled a sheer plasteel wall, her fingers finding purchase in the minute cracks and service grooves, Anya's mind replayed the chilling images from the data vault: Misha's file, the neural control device, the horrifying schematics of Project Nightingale. She could almost feel the phantom pulse of the Resonance Amplifier. It wasn't just about rescue anymore; it was about preventing a city-wide enslavement.

A Network patrol vehicle rumbled past below, its searchlights sweeping the alleys. Anya froze, pressing herself flat against the cold plasteel, her shadow melting into the deeper gloom of the wall. Her heartbeat was steady, a controlled rhythm of adrenaline and focus. Without the Spire device, her senses felt sharper, more attuned to the subtle shifts in the environment. She could hear the hum of the vehicle's engines, feel the faint vibrations of its passage, even the distant chatter of the Enforcers within.

She waited until the vehicle had passed, then continued her ascent. The wind whipped at her clothes, but she barely noticed. Her focus was absolute. She reached the first broadcast tower, a colossal spire of gleaming metal, and moved with practiced efficiency, attaching the disruptor to a critical relay junction.

As she worked, a whisper from the Spire device in her pouch felt almost palpable – a faint, insistent thrum that resonated with the city's unseen energy. It wasn't her actively using it, but a subconscious echo of its presence, a reminder of her bloodline's unique connection to the very fabric of Veridia's power. She remembered her mother, "Seer," sensing things others couldn't. Was this what it felt like? A deeper understanding of the city's pulse, its hidden vulnerabilities?

CHAPTER 22

The thought intensified her resolve. Silas might have Misha, he might have his insidious plan, but he didn't understand the true nature of the power he sought to wield. He saw it as a tool, a means of control. Anya, however, was beginning to understand it as something far more ancient, far more alive. And if she could truly tap into it, on her own terms, she could turn the Network's own strength against them. The memory of Whisper, bleeding out, fueled her, transforming grief into a cold, burning determination to strike back.

Chapter 23

Silas watched the data streams, a thin, almost imperceptible smile touching his lips. Project Chimera was ahead of schedule. Dr. Thorne's latest report confirmed the remarkable stability of Subject M's neural link to the Zenith Spire. The Resonance Cascade, the final, subtle wave of mental conditioning, was ready for deployment.

"Director, the minor neural artifact detected in Subject M's readings has resolved," Thorne's voice hummed over the intercom. "The subject's consciousness is now fully integrated with the primary resonance frequency."

Silas nodded, satisfied. Anya's foolish outburst, her desperate attempts to disrupt their progress, had been nothing but a minor irritation. The loss of her friend, a calculated move, had served its purpose, driving her to act predictably, to reveal her abilities, and ultimately, to strengthen his hand. Her mother's "Seer" abilities, once a curiosity, now made Anya and Misha key.

He turned from the main console, its holographic display showcasing a serene, perfectly ordered Veridia, devoid of conflict, its citizens moving in harmonious synchronicity. His vision. The ultimate solution to the city's inherent chaos.

"Prepare the final broadcast sequence," Silas commanded. "Synchronize the Zenith Spire with all Network broadcast towers.

CHAPTER 23

We initiate the Resonance Cascade at the designated cycle."

A chime sounded. An alert, originating from the Entertainment District. "Director, anomalous energy fluctuations detected near Sector Four's broadcast towers. Low-level interference."

Silas frowned, his thin smile vanishing. "Interference? From what source?"

"Undetermined, Director. It's... scattered. A localized energy signature, unlike any known Network technology. It appears to be designed to disrupt broad-spectrum broadcasts."

Anya. He knew it instantly. The reckless, predictable fool. She was making her moves, trying to dismantle his carefully constructed masterpiece. He scoffed. Such primitive attempts at sabotage.

"Trace the source," Silas ordered, his voice cold. "Send a rapid response unit. Neutralize the threat. And deploy a tactical drone sweep of the entire district. I want to know how she's managing this without her... little trinket." He had reviewed the test logs. Anya's proficiency without the Spire device was indeed remarkable, a testament to her inherent, inherited talents. But remarkable was not unbreakable.

He walked to the large panoramic window overlooking the city, his gaze sweeping across the neon-lit expanse. Soon, Veridia would be united, its discordant voices silenced, its chaotic desires harmonized into a single, collective will. His will.

The minor interference in the Entertainment District was a fleeting annoyance. A gnat buzzing around the architect's magnificent blueprint. He would swat it, and then he would continue building his perfect city. He allowed himself another, colder smile. Anya was still predictable. Her rage would lead her directly to him, to the Zenith Spire, to Misha. And when she arrived, he would be ready. He had already won. The Architect's vision was about to become reality.

Chapter 24

Anya cursed under her breath, the faint static on her comm unit confirming the Network's swift response. They had detected the disruptors, just as she'd known they would. Silas was moving, tightening his grip. The thought of him, calm and calculating in his sterile labs, while Misha was hooked up to his monstrous machines, sent a fresh wave of ice through her veins. She had to accelerate.

She moved with a desperate urgency, traversing the intricate, skeletal remains of old sky-bridges that crisscrossed the lower levels of the Entertainment District. This was the city's forgotten infrastructure, a silent testament to Veridia's layered history, and now her sanctuary. Her heart ached with every movement, a phantom limb where Whisper should have been, her sharp wit and tactical mind sorely missed. The grief was a dull throb, a constant companion, but it fueled her, sharpening her focus.

A sudden, high-pitched whine cut through the city's ambient hum. Anya flattened herself against the rusty girders of a collapsed bridge. A Network tactical drone, sleeker and more agile than the Vipers Seraphina had trained her against, zipped past, its optical sensors sweeping the dark crevices below. This wasn't just a simple patrol; Silas was actively hunting.

She used the broken architecture to her advantage, moving in sudden, unpredictable bursts, melting into the deeper shadows. The drone's spotlight danced across the rusted metal, always a fraction of a second behind her. Her training with Seraphina kicked in, the brutal lessons a lifeline in the desperate game of cat and mouse. She anticipated its movements, reading its flight patterns, knowing when to hold still and when to move with explosive speed.

The faint, insistent thrum from the Spire device in her pouch grew stronger, almost vibrating against her skin. It was reaching out, not actively, but resonating with the energy fluctuations of the drone, giving her a subtle edge, a whisper of information about its trajectory before her conscious mind could process it. Her mother's "Seer" abilities, a latent inheritance, were beginning to awaken, lending a precognitive edge to her movements.

She reached her final destination: a derelict broadcast repeater disguised as a defunct comm tower. Its rusted facade blended seamlessly with the urban decay, but inside, its ancient circuits still pulsed with a faint, residual power. This was the ideal spot for the last disruptor.

As she affixed the device, sealing its connections with quick, practiced movements, another thought struck her. Silas was testing Misha, amplifying the resonance for the Cascade. That resonance had to be flowing through the Network's own systems, even now, in subtle ways. If she could tap into *that* flow, perceive its pattern, she might not just disrupt it, but understand its full scope. And perhaps, find a way to sever Misha's connection from within.

The idea was audacious, incredibly dangerous. But with Whisper gone, and Misha's fate hanging in the balance, Anya knew she had to take risks. She closed her eyes, focusing past

CHAPTER 24

the physical world, pushing her consciousness towards the faint, distant hum she felt from the Zenith Spire. It was a terrifying leap of faith, an attempt to use her inherited abilities in a way she never had before, hoping to find a path through the Network's insidious plan.

Chapter 25

Silas stood before the Zenith Spire's central control hub, a towering nexus of data and energy, a satisfied smirk on his face. The Resonance Cascade was moments away from initiation. Dr. Thorne hovered nearby, meticulously running final diagnostics, his brow furrowed in concentration.

"Director, the interference in Sector Four has been neutralized," Thorne reported, his voice crisp. "The source was a series of localized disruptors. Crude, but effective enough to warrant investigation."

Silas waved a dismissive hand. "Anya Petrova. Predictable. A minor nuisance. Her frantic flailing only confirms her desperation." He watched the grand holographic display of Veridia, its lights glowing with the promise of his unified future. The citywide neural broadcast was a delicate symphony of frequencies, designed to subtly influence, to guide, to finally harmonize the fragmented minds of the populace.

"Subject M's resonance is stable and amplifying beautifully," Thorne continued, scrolling through data. "The link to the Zenith Spire is almost complete. He's ready to be the primary node for the Cascade."

Silas's smile widened. Misha was the key. His unique neural architecture, the inherited "Seer" abilities from his mother, made him the perfect conduit for the Resonance Amplifier. It was an elegance of biological design intertwined with technological genius.

"Initiate final sequence," Silas commanded, his voice filled with a chilling triumph. "Prepare for city-wide broadcast."

As the preparations began, a faint, almost imperceptible tremor ran through the control hub's massive systems. Silas felt it, a subtle shift in the energy flow, a whisper across the Network's vast infrastructure. It wasn't an anomaly, not a red flag on Thorne's diagnostics, but a *feeling*. A resonance.

He walked to a secondary console, pulling up live data on the city's unseen energy grid. His eyes, trained to spot the minutiae, searched for any deviation, any disruption. He saw the faint, localized interference from the disruptors Anya had planted – now quickly being suppressed by Network countermeasures. But beneath that, a much fainter, more subtle ripple.

It was almost imperceptible, a ghost in the machine, a resonance that shouldn't be there. It wasn't a hack, not an external attack. It felt... internal. Like a subtle resonance, *listening*.

"Thorne," Silas said, his voice unusually sharp. "Is there any secondary resonance, any... unexpected feedback from Subject M's integration?"

Thorne quickly scanned the data. "Negative, Director. All readings are within optimal parameters. The only external resonance detected was the localized interference from Sector Four, which is now being nullified."

Silas's gaze swept over the complex holographic schematics, his mind racing. Anya. Her Spire device. Her lineage. Could she be doing this? Could she be attempting to tap into the very resonance he was about to unleash? It was a bold, almost suicidal move.

He scoffed. A desperate attempt from a cornered animal. She was powerful, yes, but untrained in the true science of resonance. She was a brute force, an instinctual anomaly. His mastery of the Spire technology was absolute. He had Misha, the ultimate conduit.

"Proceed with the Cascade," Silas ordered, his voice regaining its calm, authoritative tone. "Do not delay. And have all Network surveillance actively triangulate any unusual resonance fluctuations. If Anya Petrova attempts to interfere directly with the Cascade, I want her captured immediately. Intact. I have a new purpose for her."

A new purpose. The Seer bloodline. The resonance. A chilling possibility began to form in Silas's mind, a twisted vision of controlling not just Misha, but Anya as well. He watched as the Network's central hub pulsed, ready to unleash its silent, insidious wave across Veridia. The ghost of Anya's presence was a mere oversight, a fleeting shadow in the brilliance of his impending triumph.

Chapter 26

Anya felt the city's pulse, a chaotic symphony of energy flows, amplified by the faint, insistent thrum of the Spire device in her pouch. But now, she was reaching beyond that familiar resonance, pushing her consciousness towards the Zenith Spire, towards the source of Silas's insidious broadcast. It was like trying to grasp a phantom, a whisper in the wind, but she persisted, driven by the need to understand, to counter, to save Misha.

The Network's energy grid was a complex web, a dizzying tapestry of interconnected systems. But within that chaos, Anya began to perceive a pattern, a subtle, almost rhythmic pulse that resonated with Misha's captured mind. It was a terrifying symphony of control, a carefully orchestrated flow of energy designed to subtly influence the thoughts and emotions of Veridia's populace.

As she delved deeper, using her latent Seer abilities, she felt a faint resistance, a flicker of Misha's own consciousness fighting against the overwhelming tide. It was a fragile spark, almost extinguished, but it was there. And it gave her hope.

She realized that the Network's resonance wasn't just a simple broadcast; it was a feedback loop, a complex interplay of energy flows between the Zenith Spire, Misha, and the city itself. If she could disrupt that loop, even momentarily, she might be able to create an opening, a chance to reach Misha's mind, to sever the connection.

The disruptors she had planted were a start, but they were too localized, too crude. She needed something more precise, something that could directly interfere with the resonance flow. And then she remembered the data from the Zenith Spire vault: the schematics for Project Nightingale.

She accessed the compressed data on her wrist-mounted device, the chilling diagrams of neural integration technology flashing across her vision. Within the complex schematics, she found a section detailing the resonance pathways, the specific frequencies the Network was using to control Misha.

An idea, audacious and incredibly dangerous, began to form in her mind. If she could somehow replicate those frequencies, using the Spire device, but with a counter-resonance, a disruptive echo, she might be able to create a feedback loop of her own, severing Misha's connection to the network.

It was a long shot, a desperate gamble. The Spire device was powerful, but it was also unpredictable. And attempting to directly interfere with the Network's resonance field could have catastrophic consequences. But with Misha's life on the line, and the fate of Veridia hanging in the balance, Anya knew she had no other choice.

Chapter 27

Silas watched the final preparations for the Resonance Cascade, a smug satisfaction radiating from him. The city below was poised on the brink of his grand unification. The subtle neural broadcast was already beginning, a gentle hum beneath the surface of Veridia's chaotic energy.

"Director, all broadcast towers are synchronized," Dr. Thorne reported, his voice filled with professional pride. "Subject M's resonance link is stable and amplifying. We are ready for full deployment."

Silas nodded, his gaze sweeping over the holographic display of the city. He could almost feel the subtle shift in the city's consciousness, the first tendrils of his influence reaching into the minds of its citizens. He had achieved the impossible. He had tamed Veridia.

"Begin the Resonance Cascade," Silas commanded, his voice ringing with triumph.

As the broadcast initiated, a wave of energy pulsed from the Zenith Spire, rippling outwards across the city's interconnected systems. The holographic display shimmered, the chaotic energy flows of Veridia slowly coalescing into a more ordered pattern.

Then, a flicker. A disturbance. A faint, discordant note in the symphony of his control.

Thorne's brow furrowed. "Director, we're detecting a secondary resonance. It's... it's originating from within the network itself."

Silas's smug expression vanished, replaced by a cold, calculating gaze. "Impossible. We have complete control over the resonance frequencies."

"It's... it's using the same frequencies as the Cascade, but... it's inverted," Thorne stammered, his voice laced with confusion. "It's creating a feedback loop."

On the main display, the ordered energy flows of Veridia began to flicker, disrupted by a chaotic, counter-resonance. The city lights flickered, a subtle tremor running through the very fabric of Veridia's technology.

Silas stared at the screen, his mind racing. Anya. It had to be her. She was somehow using the Spire device to interfere with his broadcast, to turn his own weapon against him.

"Isolate the source," Silas ordered, his voice tight with fury. "Sever the resonance link to Subject M. I want that connection terminated immediately."

Thorne frantically worked at his console, his fingers flying across the controls. "I can't, Director! The feedback loop is too strong. It's overriding our control protocols. Subject M's resonance is... it's amplifying the counter-signal."

Silas's eyes narrowed. Misha. Anya's brother. The key to his control, now the instrument of his downfall. She had somehow managed to tap into the very essence of the Seer bloodline, using the Spire device to amplify Misha's resistance, to turn his own power against him.

The holographic display of Veridia was now a chaotic mess of flickering lights and disrupted energy flows. The Resonance

CHAPTER 27

Cascade, his carefully orchestrated symphony of control, was crumbling around him.

Anya Petrova, the unpredictable variable, the defiant anomaly, had done the impossible. She had used his own technology, his own plan, against him. And as the city teetered on the brink of chaos, Silas felt a chilling realization dawn within him. He had underestimated her. And now, his grand vision was about to be shattered.

Chapter 28

Anya felt the chaotic surge of energy, a triumphant roar in the core of Veridia's network. The counter-resonance was working, tearing through Silas's carefully constructed Resonance Cascade. She poured all her will into the Spire device, letting it hum with a resonant frequency that amplified Misha's struggling consciousness, turning his unwilling connection into a conduit for disruption. It felt like a war within the very air, a battle for the city's mind.

But her victory was fleeting. The Spire device pulsed wildly, the effort taxing her beyond anything she had experienced before. A sharp, searing pain lanced through her head, forcing her to disengage, lest she burn out her own mind.

Just as the counter-resonance flickered, a sudden, piercing alarm echoed through the Data Pipe District. Not a Network patrol alert, but something far more insidious. A silent, urgent ping on her comm, from Jax, whose frantic fingers were still monitoring the Network's deep channels.

"Anya! He knows! Silas is sending... not Enforcers. Assassins. Elite. They're after you. All costs. They're closing in fast!" Jax's voice was a panicked hiss.

Anya didn't need to be told twice. She could feel it, a chilling presence, a cold ripple in the city's energy flows that registered even without the Spire device. These weren't standard Network forces; these were hunters, precise and lethal.

She vaulted from her precarious perch on the broadcast repeater, swinging onto a lower pipe. Her immediate surroundings were a chaotic labyrinth of metal and shadow, but it was also a death trap if she stayed. She needed to move.

The first assassin struck with terrifying speed. A dark figure, moving with impossible stealth, launched itself from a higher pipe, a shimmering energy blade materializing in its hand. Anya barely saw the attack, her instincts screaming. She twisted mid-air, a move Seraphina had drilled into her, the blade whistling past her ear, missing by a hair's breadth.

She landed hard, rolling to avoid a follow-up strike, the metallic tang of fear and adrenaline sharp in her mouth. This was different. These weren't just Network operatives; they were bred for this, for silence and death.

As she evaded, a sudden burst of energy slammed into a nearby data conduit. The pipe ruptured with a deafening shriek of tearing metal, spraying sparks and raining down scalding coolant. Below, on a busy skyway, a driver swerved violently to avoid the cascade, losing control. Their hover-car spiraled out of control, slamming into a public transport drone. A flash of light, a roar of twisting metal, and then silence. More lives lost, collateral damage in Silas's relentless pursuit.

Anya gritted her teeth, the sight fueling her rage. Each escape, each move, was costing lives.

She found a narrow maintenance ladder, leading down into the deeper, darker levels of the district, hoping to lose them in the complex under-structure. As she descended, another assassin appeared from a shadowed crevice, their eyes glowing faintly behind a sleek visor. They carried a compact railgun, its targeting laser painting a chilling red dot on the wall beside her.

Anya dropped, risking a fall, tumbling down several rungs, barely avoiding the searing projectile that tore through the metal above her head. The impact sent vibrations through the structure, dislodging rusted debris that rained down onto the squalid shanty towns built into the lower levels of the district. A section of a makeshift roof collapsed, sending terrified screams echoing up from below.

The cost. The horrifying, inescapable cost. Silas didn't care about the lives of ordinary citizens. They were expendable. Every time she fought back, every time she evaded, his rage escalated, and he unleashed more destructive power, more death. The city was bleeding, and Anya was painfully aware that her defiance was making it bleed faster.

She fled deeper into the district's forgotten corners, the hum of the Spire device a desperate pulse in her hand. She had to survive. Not just for Misha, but to stop Silas from unleashing his terror on Veridia. But the bitter truth was that every breath she took, every step she made towards saving her brother, was paid for in the lives of innocents. The blood price of her rebellion was rising, and she knew, with a chilling certainty, that it would only get higher.

Chapter 29

Silas watched the live feed from the Data Pipe District, his expression a chilling mixture of controlled fury and intellectual fascination. The Resonance Cascade was still flickering, a testament to Anya's stubborn, instinctive interference. But her counter-resonance was weakening, just as he predicted. And his assassins were closing in.

"Director, the primary assassination unit has confirmed engagement," a technician reported, his voice crisp. "Subject Petrova is demonstrating remarkable evasive capabilities. Unit Delta incurred minor damage from debris caused by a high-impact projectile."

Silas barely registered the damage report. His gaze was fixed on the tactical overlay, showing Anya's frantic movements through the maze of conduits and decaying structures. He saw the bursts of energy, the collapses, the flickering indicators of civilian casualties. A calculated, acceptable price.

"Increase the pressure," Silas commanded, his voice a low growl. "Deploy additional units. I want her contained. Alive, if possible, but if not... the Spire device is the priority."

He turned to Dr. Thorne, who was meticulously reviewing the latest data from Misha's neural readings. "The counter-resonance, Thorne. What is its source? Is it purely organic, or is she consciously manipulating the device?"

Thorne adjusted his glasses. "It's a fascinating anomaly, Director. The Spire device is amplifying her inherent neural resonance, acting as a feedback loop. Her 'Seer' abilities, combined with the artifact, are creating a disruptive frequency. It's highly unstable, but effective."

Silas's eyes narrowed. "Unstable. Good. It cannot be sustained. She is burning herself out, pushing the limits of her organic form. My analysis was correct. She is a brute, without the finesse of true control."

He looked back at the live feed. Anya was a small, fleeting shadow against the backdrop of destruction. He saw the civilian hover-car crash, the collapsing roofs in the lower levels. The incidental casualties were merely proof of the force he was bringing to bear. The city was a machine, and sometimes, cogs broke.

"Director, the Resonance Cascade is stabilizing," Thorne announced, a note of relief in his voice. "The counter-resonance is fading. Subject M's integration is proceeding as planned."

Silas allowed himself a tight, grim smile. Anya's desperate attempt had been futile. She had merely delayed the inevitable, and in doing so, she had revealed the extent of her capabilities, and her vulnerabilities. She was a valuable specimen, but a wild, untamed one. He would simply have to break her.

He turned from the screens, his gaze fixed on the glowing blue core of the Zenith Spire, pulsing with the power that would soon envelop Veridia. "The city will submit. One way or another. And Anya Petrova... she will either join the symphony, or she will be crushed beneath it."

His unseen hand reached out, deploying more assets, tightening the net. The assassins were merely the first wave. He knew

CHAPTER 29

Anya's attachment to the people of Veridia, to the struggling masses she claimed to protect. He would use that against her. Every death, every shattered life in her wake, would be a message. A testament to the futility of resistance. And eventually, she would break. Or she would be broken.

Chapter 30

The screech of tearing metal and the distant cries from below fueled Anya's desperate flight. The Data Pipe District, once a place of relative sanctuary, had become a deadly playground for Silas's assassins. They moved with a chilling precision, their energy weapons singing through the air, forcing Anya into increasingly desperate maneuvers.

Her initial burst of counter-resonance had faded, the Spire device now a dull weight against her side. The headache hammered behind her eyes, a sharp reminder of the toll of pushing her inherited abilities. She couldn't risk another direct interference; she needed to survive.

A shadow detached itself from the labyrinthine pipes above her. Anya's senses screamed a warning. She spun, dropping into a low crouch as an assassin, a blurred shape against the neon-lit sky, landed silently where she had been a moment before. Its hands, tipped with razor-sharp vibro-blades, swept through the air, carving arcs of light.

Anya rolled, coming up against a thick, rusted girder. She used it as a pivot, kicking out with a desperate lunge. Her boot connected with the assassin's knee, eliciting a guttural grunt. It staggered back, its movements momentarily disrupted.

This was Seraphina's training: brutal, direct, and focused on exploiting weaknesses. Anya followed up, not with finesse, but with pure, unadulterated fury. She slammed her elbow into the assassin's visor, cracking the hardened plasteel. The assassin recoiled, momentarily blinded.

But they were relentless. Another figure, cloaked in dark, form-fitting armor, emerged from the shadows, its railgun already charging. Anya didn't hesitate. She threw herself sideways, clinging to a thin pipe that ran horizontally across a dizzying chasm. The railgun slug tore through the air where she had been, impacting the girder with a violent *clang* that echoed for miles.

The impact sent vibrations through the structure, causing a cascade effect. Below, in a bustling cargo hub, a towering stack of synth-steel shipping containers, destabilized by the tremors, began to topple. The grinding roar was deafening, followed by the crunch of metal and the distant, muffled screams of dock workers caught beneath the collapsing mountain of cargo.

Anya saw it all from her precarious perch, the new deaths painting a horrifying picture. Each time she evaded, each time she survived, Silas inflicted more suffering on the city. It was a twisted game, designed to break her, to make her responsible for the very destruction she fought against.

Her heart pounded, not just from exertion, but from a cold, bitter hatred. This wasn't just about escape anymore. It was about making Silas pay for every single life lost.

She scrambled along the pipe, the assassins closing in, their movements fluid and coordinated. She needed to lose them, to find a place to regroup, to plan her next move. The Data Pipe District was her sanctuary, but it was becoming a graveyard.

She spotted an access hatch, half-hidden beneath a tangle of defunct wiring. It led to a lower service level, a warren of cramped, unlit tunnels. It was a gamble, a dive into the unknown, but it was better than staying exposed.

With a final desperate burst of speed, Anya reached the hatch, kicking it open with a desperate surge of adrenaline. As she slipped inside, she heard the *thud* of the assassins landing on the pipe behind her, their low, guttural curses echoing in the confined space. They were right behind her. The ghost in the girders had found a new hiding place, but the hunt was far from over.

Chapter 31

Silas watched the cascading destruction on his main display, a cold satisfaction spreading across his features. Anya was proving to be a remarkably resilient pest, but each evasion cost her, and the city, dearly. The collapsing containers in the cargo hub, the terrified screams echoing from the Data Pipe District's lower levels – all calculated collateral.

"Director, the primary assassination unit has confirmed Subject Petrova has entered the service tunnels of the Data Pipe District," Thorne reported, his voice a drone. "We have limited visibility in those sections, but Unit Sigma is tracking her thermal signature."

Silas steepled his fingers, his gaze fixed on the flickering heat signature on the tactical overlay. "Excellent. Confine her. The tunnels are a maze, but they are also a cage. She cannot escape the district now. Deploy gas-phase dampeners to key egress points. Force her into the open, or into a cul-de-sac."

He allowed himself a moment of grim amusement. Anya believed she was fighting for Veridia. In reality, she was merely accelerating its transformation. Every life lost, every disruption, would only strengthen the public's desire for order, for the unified consciousness he offered. His Resonance Cascade was slowly but surely stabilizing, despite her desperate interference.

Misha's compliance, though briefly rattled, was absolute.

"Director, analysis confirms continued residual interference from Subject Petrova's Spire device," Thorne interrupted, his brow furrowed. "It's weak, but it's still acting as a minor disruptive element to the Cascade's lowest frequencies."

Silas scoffed. "A dying gasp. Her organic limitations will eventually overpower her ability to harness the artifact's true power. She is merely an uncontrolled variable. A fascinating one, but ultimately, disposable."

He walked to the panoramic window, looking out over the city. Below, the Data Pipe District looked like a scarred, industrial ruin, but to Silas, it was merely another chessboard. Anya was attempting to hide in the shadows, but he controlled the light.

"What is the projected casualty count from the latest incident, Thorne?" Silas asked, his voice flat.

Thorne glanced at a side screen. "Estimates suggest minimal civilian loss, Director. Three fatalities, seventeen injured, mostly industrial workers. Infrastructure damage is significant."

"Acceptable," Silas murmured. "The city will adapt. It will crave stability. And I will provide it. Anya Petrova's defiance is a temporary inconvenience. A final, desperate dance before the music truly begins."

He turned back to the tactical map, his eyes gleaming with a cold, predatory intelligence. "Focus all available surveillance on the service tunnels. Initiate sound dampeners in those sections. I want her disoriented. Cut off. And ensure the assassination units have full authorization for lethal force if she resists capture."

Silas smiled, a chilling, triumphant expression. He had Anya cornered. The service tunnels would be her tomb, or her cage.

CHAPTER 31

And when he finally had her, he would extract every last secret of her Seer bloodline. Then, the Resonance Cascade would truly begin, and Veridia would finally be

Chapter 32

The service tunnels were a suffocating nightmare of tight spaces and echoing darkness. Anya moved through them like a ghost, her senses heightened by the constant threat of Silas's assassins. The air was thick with the scent of stagnant water and ozone, the only sounds the drip of condensation and the distant hum of machinery. Her ribs ached, a persistent reminder of Silas's brutal kick, but she ignored it, focusing on the faint, almost imperceptible vibrations that told her of approaching footsteps.

The sound dampeners Silas had deployed turned the tunnels into a terrifying void. Anya relied on her enhanced hearing, catching the subtle shift in air currents, the faint scrape of armor against concrete. Her training with Seraphina had taught her to trust her instincts, to become part of the shadow.

She found herself in a wider conduit, the main artery of the tunnel system. A Network assassin, its visor glowing faintly in the gloom, stepped out from a cross-section, its energy blade already drawn. This one was faster, more agile than the others she'd faced.

Anya didn't hesitate. She launched herself forward, not towards the assassin, but to a dangling cluster of thick data cables. She swung, using her momentum to kick off the wall and launch herself over the assassin's head. As she passed, she lashed out with a coiled length of discarded wiring she'd picked up, wrapping it around the assassin's neck.

The assassin gurgled, its hands flying to its throat, momentarily distracted. Anya landed behind it, pulling on the wire with all her might, using the tunnel wall as leverage. The assassin thrashed, its powerful limbs flailing, but Anya held fast, remembering Seraphina's grim lessons on chokeholds. The assassin's movements grew weaker, its glowing eyes dimming.

Then, a new threat. Another assassin dropped from a high access shaft, its railgun already aimed. Anya saw the red dot appear on the wall just inches from her head. She abandoned her chokehold, pushing off the weakened assassin and rolling into a narrow crevice as the railgun fired. The slug tore through the air, hitting the first assassin squarely in the back, sending a spray of sparks and a sickening crunch of shattered armor. The assassin crumpled, inert.

Anya's heart pounded. She was alive, but at a terrible cost. More deaths. Each time, the collateral damage grew. Her defiance was painting the city red.

She crawled deeper into the crevice, hearing the new assassin clambering down the access shaft. She knew she couldn't stay here. Silas was relentless, and these tunnels, while offering temporary concealment, were ultimately a trap. She needed to get back to the surface, to the chaos of the city where she could use its sprawling expanse to her advantage. The thirst for revenge against Silas was a burning fire within her, pushing her forward despite the mounting losses.

Chapter 33

Silas watched Anya's heat signature flicker across the tactical display, a tiny, defiant ember in the vast darkness of the Data Pipe District's service tunnels. His lips curled into a cold smile. She was resourceful, he would give her that. But even the most resourceful prey eventually tired.

"Director, Assassin Unit Four reports neutralizing Unit Three," Thorne's voice hummed over the intercom. "They are resuming pursuit of Subject Petrova."

"Good," Silas murmured. "She is a testament to the resilience of the human spirit, an admirable, if ultimately futile, defiance." He looked at the live feed, seeing the chaotic energy readings caused by the recent collateral damage. The collapsing containers, the ruptured pipes. Just more evidence of her destructive nature, her inability to grasp the concept of order.

The Resonance Cascade continued its subtle, insidious work. Thorne's diagnostics showed it was stabilizing, slowly but surely overcoming Anya's initial disruptive surge. Misha's neural readings were optimal, his mind a quiet, receptive conduit.

"The Seer bloodline is undeniably powerful," Silas mused aloud, more to himself than to Thorne. "An untapped resource. Such a shame it has been so... mismanaged by its previous custodians." He envisioned Anya, stripped of her defiance, her powerful resonance controlled, integrated into his grand design alongside her brother. A perfectly ordered, infinitely valuable asset.

His gaze returned to the tactical map. Anya was heading deeper into the older, unmapped sections of the tunnels. A calculated move, or a desperate one? He preferred to believe the latter. Desperation led to mistakes.

"Activate Phase Two containment protocols for the Data Pipe District's lower levels," Silas commanded. "Flood sectors Gamma-7 through Gamma-12 with sonic dampeners. Seal off all known surface egress points in the immediate vicinity. And deploy low-frequency sonic emitters within those tunnels. We will flush her out."

Thorne executed the commands with practiced efficiency. The holographic map of the tunnels began to glow with new, red-tinted zones, indicating the areas of intensified sonic pressure and sealed exits. It was a net, tightening around its prey.

"Director, the emitters will cause significant disorientation to organic life forms," Thorne noted, a hint of caution in his voice.

"Precisely," Silas replied, his voice devoid of empathy. "She will be confused, vulnerable. She cannot hide from sound. The tunnels will become her labyrinth. And when she emerges, she will be ready for capture."

He watched the map, the anticipation growing. Anya Petrova was a symbol of chaos, of the untamed human element he sought to suppress. Capturing her, breaking her, would be a final, poignant victory. The Architect's net was closing. And soon, the only sound in Veridia would be the harmonious hum of his unified city.

Chapter 34

The low-frequency sonic emitters hit Anya like a physical blow. A relentless, agonizing pressure built in her skull, vibrating through her teeth and bones. It was a disorienting, nauseating assault that stole her balance and blurred her vision. The tunnels, already a suffocating maze, became a nightmarish sensory deprivation chamber.

She stumbled, slamming against the cold concrete wall, the headache intensifying into a blinding agony. The assassins, their movements unaffected by the emitters, advanced. She could feel their presence, a chilling pressure in the ringing void, even if her eyes struggled to focus.

Anya desperately clutched the Spire device, its faint hum a fragile counterpoint to the sonic assault. She tried to push back, to use her inherent resonance, but the emitters were too strong, overpowering her connection, making her head throb with unbearable pain. She was isolated, cut off, her senses failing.

Then, through the haze of agony, she heard it – a faint, almost imperceptible *scrape* of metal. Not the assassins. Something else. Something above her.

It was Boris. And Seraphina.

A section of the old tunnel ceiling above Anya shuddered, a

thin sliver of light appearing as Boris, his face grim, used a portable cutting torch to breach the reinforced concrete. The roaring hiss of the torch provided a momentary, painful respite from the sonic pressure.

"Anya! Grab on!" Boris yelled, his voice strained.

Anya forced her trembling hands upwards, her fingers brushing against the rough edge of a heavy-duty cable Boris lowered through the gap. Just as she secured her grip, an assassin burst from the shadows behind her, its vibro-blade arcing towards her back.

"Go!" Seraphina's voice cut through the air, sharp and urgent. She appeared at the opening, her own energy weapon spitting fire, creating a defensive barrier.

Anya pulled, her muscles screaming in protest against the sonic pressure and the lingering pain of her broken ribs. Boris hauled her up, his powerful arms straining. As Anya scrambled through the narrow opening, the sound of energy fire intensified below, Seraphina engaging the assassins directly.

She collapsed onto a narrow, hidden ledge, gasping for air, the sonic assault finally receding as they ascended higher into the city's forgotten spaces. Below, the fighting continued, the flashes of energy fire illuminating the tight tunnel network.

"We heard the sonic emitters," Boris grunted, pulling her further back into a shadowed alcove. "Seraphina knew Silas was going to try to flush you out. We've been tracking Network comms."

Anya looked back, her heart wrenching. Seraphina, the brutal, pragmatic leader of the Crimson Hand, was risking her life to hold off Silas's elite killers, buying Anya precious time. The line between allies and enemies, once so clear, was blurring into a painful gray. They were still fighting, but the cost was astronomical. Every single escape, every battle, brought more death, more destruction to the city she was trying to save.

Chapter 35

Silas watched the tactical display, a vein throbbing faintly at his temple. The sonic dampeners and emitters should have rendered Anya helpless, yet her heat signature was now ascending vertically, a frustrating anomaly in his meticulously crafted net.

"Director, analysis confirms a breach in Sector Delta-9," Dr. Thorne reported, his voice tinged with alarm. "Unauthorized ascent. It appears to be a direct extraction by a third party. Energy signatures consistent with Crimson Hand weaponry."

Silas slammed his fist against the console, a rare display of raw anger. "The Crimson Hand! They are interfering with my capture. Their audacity is... infuriating."

He had pushed Anya into a corner, forced her into a desperate situation. He had accounted for her resilience, her innate abilities, even her reliance on that antiquated Spire device. But he had not fully anticipated the intervention of Seraphina and her crude but effective thugs. Their presence was a wild card, a chaotic element he had failed to fully contain.

"Increase aerial patrols over Sector Delta," Silas commanded, his voice cold and sharp. "Deploy high-altitude thermal scanners. I want that transport intercepted. And trace the origin point of that breach. Find out how the Crimson Hand knew her location. Their internal network must have been compromised."

He returned his attention to the Resonance Cascade. Despite Anya's brief disruption, the city-wide neural broadcast was largely stable, steadily progressing. Misha's resonance was strong, fully integrated, his mind a quiet, compliant conduit. The minor setback with Anya was merely a delay, a fleeting interruption in his grand design.

"The populace is showing increased compliance in test sectors, Director," Thorne reported, a note of satisfaction returning to his voice. "The neural pathways are adapting. The Cascade is achieving its desired effect."

Silas allowed a thin, cruel smile to return to his lips. Even as Anya struggled, as lives were lost in her wake, his ultimate victory was inevitable. The chaotic actions of the Crimson Hand, the desperate struggles of Anya Petrova – they were merely accelerating the city's desire for order, for the peace only he could offer.

He looked at the tactical display, seeing the small dot that was Anya's escaping heat signature moving across the higher levels of the Data Pipe District. He knew she would continue to fight, to rage against the inevitable. But every desperate act, every life lost, only served to strengthen his hand. The city was bleeding, and soon, it would beg for the surgeon. And Silas, the architect of its new reality, would be there to answer.

Chapter 36

Anya burst into Seraphina's temporary safe house, a utilitarian space buried deep beneath a forgotten industrial complex, her lungs burning, her body aching with residual pain. The low-frequency emitters still echoed in her ears, a phantom throb behind her eyes. Boris was already there, grim-faced, securing the entrance. Seraphina stood in the center of the room, her gaze sharp, assessing Anya's battered state.

"You made it," Seraphina stated, not a question, not a welcome, just a cold observation. "The Network is in a frenzy. Your disruptors, combined with that surge... it rattled them."

Anya slammed her fist onto a nearby crate, the wood splintering under the force. "Rattled them? They sent assassins! They filled the tunnels with those damn emitters! They killed more innocents trying to get to me!" Her voice was raw, laced with fury. "And Jax... he's why Whisper is dead, Seraphina. You knew he'd been compromised before, and you still used him."

Seraphina's eyes narrowed, a flicker of something akin to defensiveness in their depths. "We take calculated risks, Petrova. Jax's intel was invaluable. The Network has leverage on everyone."

"Leverage that cost Whisper her life!" Anya retorted, stepping closer, her gaze unwavering. "And it almost cost me mine.

Your 'calculated risks' are just a convenient excuse for collateral damage. We need to cut him loose. Now."

Seraphina held her gaze, a long, tense moment of silence passing between them. Then, surprisingly, she nodded. "He's too much of a liability now that Silas knows. He's a broken link. Boris, relocate Jax to the lowest levels. Strip his comms. He'll work, but he's off the network. No more intel from him."

Boris nodded, turning to carry out the order without a word. Anya felt a bitter satisfaction. It wasn't true justice for Whisper, but it was something. A small victory in a world of crushing defeats.

"So, what now, 'Ghost'?" Seraphina asked, using the new nickname with a hint of grim acknowledgement. "Silas knows you know. He's tightening his grip on the city. The Resonance Cascade is still progressing, even if you managed to delay it."

Anya paced, her mind racing. The Project Nightingale data, the miniature Resonance Amplifier she'd seen in the vault, Misha's role as the primary node, the horrifying idea of an entire city's mind being subtly controlled. It all converged on one undeniable truth: the Zenith Spire was the key.

"We go to the Zenith Spire," Anya declared, her voice firm. "We hit him where he's most vulnerable. We rescue Misha. And we stop the Resonance Cascade before it's too late."

Seraphina raised an eyebrow. "Direct assault? That's suicide. The Spire is the most heavily fortified location in Veridia. And after your last visit, it will be bristling with defenses, expecting you."

"We won't go in guns blazing," Anya countered, a cold fire in her eyes. "We use what we have. We use his own plan against him. He's using Misha to amplify the Cascade, to control the city. What if we use that same link... to break it? To make the

Network's resonance turn against itself?"

A dangerous glint appeared in Seraphina's eyes. "A risky gamble. But the Crimson Hand thrives on chaos. And if you can sever the Network's control, the city will be ripe for... liberation." She didn't specify *her* brand of liberation, but Anya understood. This was still an alliance of convenience, forged in the fires of shared enmity, but fundamentally different goals.

"We need more than disruptors," Anya continued. "We need to understand the resonance. The Spire device can do more than just amplify. It can manipulate. My mother... she was a Seer. She could *perceive* the energy. Maybe I can do more than just disrupt. Maybe I can reverse it."

Seraphina regarded Anya for a long moment, then a slow, predatory smile spread across her scarred face. "Alright, Ghost. We'll give you your shot. The Network will never expect us to hit the Spire again so soon. And if you can turn their own weapon on them... that would be quite a show. Let's make Silas pay."

The alliance was shifting, becoming more volatile, more dangerous. Anya was stepping further into the brutal world of the Crimson Hand, using their resources, their methods, for her own desperate goal. She was no longer just running; she was hunting. And the target was Silas.

Chapter 37

Silas stood before the vast panoramic window of his Zenith Spire office, watching the neon glow of Veridia. The recent skirmish in the Data Pipe District, the frustrating escape of Anya Petrova, had been a minor inconvenience. Her crude disruptors had caused a momentary ripple, but the Resonance Cascade, his magnum opus, was now humming along smoothly.

"Director, the Resonance Cascade is at seventy-three percent integration," Dr. Thorne announced, his voice filled with quiet triumph. "Neural compliance in target sectors is exceeding projections. The city is... accepting."

Silas allowed himself a thin smile. "Excellent, Doctor. Anya Petrova's foolish rebellion only served to accelerate the process. The more chaos she wrought, the more the populace craved order. She played directly into my hands."

He observed the tactical display, showing the current status of all Network assets. His assassins were being debriefed, their failure to capture Anya a temporary setback. He would simply send more, better equipped. He was already planning for her inevitable, desperate move towards the Zenith Spire. She would come for her brother. And he would be waiting.

"The residual counter-resonance from Subject Petrova's Spire device is now almost entirely suppressed," Thorne continued. "Her organic limitations are clear. She cannot sustain that level of interference for long."

Silas nodded, a flicker of cold satisfaction in his eyes. He had known her weakness. Her raw, untamed power was a double-edged sword, taxing her own physical and mental limits. He, however, wielded power with scientific precision, with perfect control.

"And Subject M?" Silas inquired, his gaze drifting to the separate, shielded display of Misha's vital signs. "Is his amplification stable? Is he ready for the final, full-spectrum broadcast?"

"Stable and optimal, Director," Thorne confirmed. "His neural architecture, as a member of the 'Seer' lineage, is uniquely suited for this role. He is the perfect, compliant conduit."

Silas turned from the window, his gaze sweeping over the array of complex machinery and holographic displays in his command center. "Prepare for the final phase of the Resonance Cascade. At ninety-five percent integration, we will initiate the full-spectrum broadcast. Veridia will be completely unified. All dissent, all chaos, all unpredictable variables... will cease to exist."

He considered Anya Petrova. Her desperation, her grief, her growing ruthlessness. She was a dangerous, unpredictable element. But he had foreseen her every move. He had anticipated her emotional reaction, her desire for revenge. He knew she would come to the Spire. And he would use her predictable actions to his ultimate advantage.

"Enhance all defensive protocols for the Zenith Spire," Silas commanded. "Triple internal patrols. Activate perimeter energy shields to maximum. No unauthorized entry. And prepare for a direct confrontation with Anya Petrova and any Crimson Hand elements she brings with her. I want live feeds from every sector of the Spire. Every movement. Every breath."

Silas's lips curved into a chilling smile. The final act was about to begin. Anya Petrova believed she was hunting him, that she was striking at his core. But in truth, she was merely walking into the next phase of his meticulously planned victory. He would not just defeat her; he would absorb her, control her, and her unique Seer abilities would be seamlessly integrated into the very Resonance Cascade she sought to destroy. Veridia would finally be complete, and Anya Petrova, the last bastion of chaos, would be neutralized.

Chapter 38

The air in Seraphina's hidden bunker crackled with a volatile mix of desperation and cold resolve. Anya, her eyes burning with a relentless fire, stared at the holographic map of the Zenith Spire, its imposing structure a defiant monument to Silas's power. The grief for Whisper, the fury at Jax's betrayal, the escalating collateral damage – it had all coalesced into a single, unshakeable purpose.

"Silas dies," Anya stated, her voice low and utterly devoid of emotion. It wasn't a threat; it was a vow, carved from the bedrock of her pain. "He won't just be stopped. He will pay for Misha. For Whisper. For every life he's crushed under his heel."

Seraphina, leaning against a reinforced wall, crossed her arms. "Revenge is a powerful motivator, Ghost. Just make sure it doesn't blind you. The Spire is a fortress. And the Network is reacting."

Just then, Boris's voice, strained and urgent, crackled over their comms. "We've got movement! Network forces, heavy deployment, converging on Sector Three. They're making a push. And the Resonance Cascade... it's intensifying."

Anya felt it, a subtle shift in the air, a faint, almost imperceptible hum that resonated in the deepest parts of her mind. It was the Cascade, working its insidious magic. She focused, using her Seer abilities, and the invisible hum resolved into a dizzying array of frequencies, weaving through the city. She could feel the faint, insidious whispers in the minds of the citizens – a calming presence, a suggestion of unity, a gentle push towards compliance. It was working. Silas's weapon was active.

"They're coming for us," Seraphina said, pushing off the wall. "Silas is trying to eliminate all threats before the Cascade is complete. We need to move. Now."

The confrontation came swiftly, deep within the winding, abandoned tunnels beneath the industrial complex. Network Enforcers, their energy weapons blazing, stormed their position. The fighting was brutal, a desperate melee in the confined spaces. Anya, a blur of motion, disarmed and neutralized with deadly efficiency, her training with Seraphina paying dividends. Each strike was precise, every movement economical.

Seraphina fought with a ferocious intensity, her energy blade carving arcs of destruction through the Enforcers. She was a whirlwind of calculated violence, a true force to be reckoned with. But the Network's forces were overwhelming, relentless.

As Anya dispatched an Enforcer with a swift, bone-jarring kick, a searing energy blast ripped through the air, hitting Seraphina in the shoulder. She cried out, staggering back, her energy blade clattering to the ground. A crimson stain bloomed rapidly on her dark combat suit.

"Seraphina!" Anya yelled, rushing to her side.

"Keep going, Ghost!" Seraphina grunted, clutching her shoulder, her face pale but defiant. "They can't get to the Spire if they're fighting us here. Go! Make him pay!"

Anya felt a surge of cold terror, mixed with a bitter resolve. Another one, injured, falling. It was happening again. But this time, she wouldn't let it stop her. She couldn't.

CHAPTER 38

She made eye contact with Seraphina, a silent understanding passing between them. With a final, desperate look, Anya turned, melting into the deeper shadows of the tunnels, leaving the wounded leader of the Crimson Hand to hold the line.

As she fled, the pervasive hum of the Resonance Cascade grew stronger. She glimpsed it in the flickering emergency lights filtering from the streets above: a pedestrian, usually agitated, now walked with a placid, almost vacant expression; a group of rioters, their anger previously palpable, now seemed listless, their shouts dying into murmurs of vague contentment. The city was changing, its vibrant chaos subtly fading into a disturbing tranquility. Silas's influence was taking root, turning Veridia into a silent, obedient collective. Anya knew she was running out of time. Her vow to kill Silas was no longer just a personal vendetta; it was the only way to save Veridia from a fate worse than death.

Chapter 39

Silas watched the tactical displays in the Zenith Spire, a triumphant smile spreading across his face. The Network's forces were engaging the remnants of the Crimson Hand in Sector Three, pinning them down. And Seraphina, the audacious leader, was wounded. Excellent.

"Director, the Resonance Cascade has reached ninety-eight percent integration," Dr. Thorne announced, his voice almost reverent. "Neural compliance is nearly total. The city... is one."

Silas turned, his gaze sweeping across the holographic map of Veridia. The chaotic energy flows of the city were now perfectly synchronized, a harmonious, unified pulse. He could almost feel the collective consciousness, the millions of individual minds gently guided into a single, compliant entity. His vision was complete.

"Initiate full-spectrum broadcast," Silas commanded, his voice filled with a chilling finality. "The last two percent will simply be an affirmation. Veridia is ours."

As the command was executed, a wave of profound calm settled over the control hub. The city outside, seen through the panoramic window, shimmered with a new, subtle luminescence. Public screens that had once displayed a cacophony of news and advertisements now showed serene, flowing patterns, accompanied by a low, comforting hum. On the ground level, citizens moved with a quiet, purposeful rhythm, their faces tranquil, their hurried steps replaced by a gentle, unhurried glide.

"Exceptional, Director," Thorne breathed, awe in his voice. "The Resonance Cascade is fully active. Veridia is now... in harmony."

Silas felt a surge of unparalleled satisfaction. Decades of planning, years of research, countless obstacles, all culminating in this moment. The world's first truly unified metropolis.

Then, an alert flickered on his personal console. A high-priority signal, bypassing standard Network comms. An Assassin Unit, not from his primary force, but a specialized, autonomous unit, trained for deep infiltration and silent elimination.

"Director, a rogue signature detected within the Zenith Spire's outer access tunnels," a secondary technician reported, his voice tinged with surprise. "It's... Subject Petrova. She's moving fast. She bypassed the perimeter sensors."

Silas's triumphant smile faltered, a flicker of irritation crossing his face. Anya. The persistent, unpredictable variable. He had assumed she would be pinned down with the Crimson Hand, or at least heavily wounded.

"Impossible," Thorne mumbled, checking his own diagnostics. "How could she penetrate the Spire's outer defenses unnoticed? The perimeter shields are at maximum."

Silas recovered quickly, his irritation giving way to a cold, calculating resolve. "She is using her Spire device, her inherent Seer abilities. It's the only explanation. She found a blind spot, a resonance distortion too subtle for our conventional sensors."

He pulled up a tactical overlay of the Spire's internal structure, his gaze narrowing on Anya's rapidly advancing heat signature. She was making a direct line for the central core, for Misha. Predictable.

"Deploy Assassin Unit Seven," Silas commanded, his voice sharp. "Activate all internal security drones in her sector. Route her through Sector Gamma-9 – the 'Glass Maze.' And authorize lethal force. I want her terminated. She has become an unacceptable risk. The Cascade is too important to be disrupted now. Bring me her Spire device, and if she resists, bring me her head."

His eyes gleamed with a chilling resolve. The city was unified. His grand vision was complete. Anya Petrova was merely the last, defiant echo of a past he was determined to erase. He watched her relentless pursuit, knowing that this time, there would be no escape. The Architect's triumph would be absolute.

Chapter 40

Anya moved through the Zenith Spire's "Glass Maze," a terrifying expanse of transparent plasteel walkways suspended over dizzying chasms, each step echoing through the vast, sterile space. The air hummed with the oppressive silence of Silas's unified city, the subtle, pervasive presence of the Resonance Cascade pressing in on her mind. But beneath the surface, a new terror bloomed – a chilling awareness of the Network's elite assassins, moving like phantoms within the transparent walls.

Her Spire device thrummed, a desperate counter-pulse against the Cascade, a fragile tether to her own thoughts. Her Seer abilities, sharpened by desperation, gave her a fleeting glimpse of shimmering heat signatures, of subtle distortions in the glass that betrayed the assassins' presence. They weren't just hunting her; they were toying with her, guiding her deeper into the maze.

Suddenly, a shimmer. An assassin materialized from the transparency, its vibro-blade arcing. Anya ducked, the blade slicing through the air where her head had been. She parried with a salvaged plasteel rod, the clang reverberating through the glass. Her movements were fluid, precise, a testament to Seraphina's brutal training, but the assassin was faster, stronger, its every strike imbued with lethal intent.

She fought, a desperate dance on the precipice of a thousand-meter drop. The transparency of the floor beneath her feet was a constant, dizzying reminder of her vulnerability. More assassins appeared, their silent forms weaving through the glass, cutting off her escape routes. Anya was trapped, caught in Silas's glittering web.

Just as an assassin lunged, its blade aimed for her heart, a faint, almost imperceptible hum resonated in Anya's mind. It wasn't the Spire device. It was Misha. A desperate echo of his consciousness, fighting against the overwhelming resonance, a whisper of connection through the mental fog. He was still in there. Still fighting.

The whisper of Misha's resistance ignited a fresh surge of power within Anya. She pushed, consciously, against the pervasive hum of the Cascade, pouring her will into a single, desperate prayer. The Spire device flared, a brilliant blue light briefly illuminating the Glass Maze. It wasn't a direct attack, but a surge of raw, untamed energy that resonated with Misha's own defiant pulse.

The Network assassins staggered, their visors momentarily flickering, their movements jerky. It was a fraction of a second, an opening. Anya seized it. She launched herself at the nearest assassin, disarming it with a brutal efficiency, then used its own momentum to send it hurtling backwards, slamming into another. The transparent wall cracked, web-like fissures spreading from the impact.

The assassins recovered quickly, their cold fury renewed. But Anya had found her purpose, her path. Misha was fighting. She had to reach him. The glass maze was no longer a trap; it was a path to her brother, and to Silas.

Chapter 41

Silas watched the live feed from the Glass Maze, his fingers drumming a frustrated rhythm on the console. Anya Petrova was an infuriating anomaly. Her resilience was unmatched, her ability to exploit even the tiniest crack in his flawless designs truly astonishing.

"Director, the secondary resonance from Subject Petrova has flared again," Dr. Thorne reported, his voice tight. "It's impacting local Network security protocols. Minor disruptions to automated patrols in Sector Gamma."

Silas scoffed. "Minor. A desperate surge. She cannot sustain it. Her primitive connection to the Spire artifact is inefficient. It taxes her, weakens her. She will burn out before she reaches the core."

Yet, a flicker of unease gnawed at him. He had designed Project Chimera, designed the Resonance Cascade, to be flawless. Misha's mind, a Seer lineage amplified by his implant, was supposed to be a perfectly compliant conduit. But Anya, the other half of that lineage, was proving to be a persistent, unexpected variable. Her raw, untamed power, fueled by emotion, was a chaotic element he struggled to quantify, to control.

"Assassin Unit Seven reports direct engagement within the Glass Maze," another technician interjected. "Subject Petrova is demonstrating extreme combat proficiency. Two units neutralized."

Silas's eyes narrowed, a muscle twitching in his jaw. Two units. His elite assassins. Dispatched by a single, unaugmented woman. This was beyond mere street fighting. She was evolving, adapting at an alarming rate.

He pulled up the tactical overlay, seeing Anya's heat signature relentlessly pushing deeper into the Spire, towards the central core. She was like a single, determined virus, burrowing into the heart of his machine.

"Activate Level Four containment protocols for the Glass Maze," Silas commanded, his voice cold and precise. "Seal all egress points. Flood the entire section with nerve agent at maximum concentration. Lethal dosage. She will be neutralized, or she will die attempting to escape. I will not have her disrupt the final stages of the Cascade."

Thorne looked up, his face paling. "Director, the nerve agent... it's designed for rapid neural shutdown. It will impact all organic life in the sector. Including our own units if they are not evacuated immediately."

"A necessary sacrifice," Silas stated, his gaze unyielding. "The Resonance Cascade is too vital. The purity of the unified consciousness cannot be compromised. Evacuate all remaining Network personnel from the Glass Maze immediately. The assassins have their orders. They will complete their mission or perish."

He watched the timer count down, the red zone of the nerve agent spreading across the holographic map. He would eradicate this unpredictable variable, this chaotic element, once and for all. He had created a perfect system, a perfect city. And nothing, not even the raw power of a Seer, would be allowed to crack its flawless façade. The Architect's vision was on the brink of absolute completion, and he would not permit any further interference.

Chapter 42

Anya felt the subtle shift in the air, a metallic tang, a faint, sweet smell that tickled her nostrils – nerve agent. Silas wasn't just trapping her; he was actively trying to kill her. The Glass Maze, once a challenge, had become a death chamber. The few remaining assassins were now a grim secondary threat, their movements accelerating, knowing their own time was running out.

She had to get out. Now.

Her eyes scanned the transparent walls, her mind racing. The cracks from the earlier impact, the faint tremors from the nerve agent's release, combined with the subtle hum of the Cascade and her own Seer senses, painted a chaotic but strangely insightful picture. The Spire device thrummed against her, resonating with a desperate urgency.

She focused, pushing her consciousness, not just to disrupt, but to *perceive*. The Network's energy grid, the very arteries of the Spire, pulsed with a rhythm. And within that rhythm, a subtle vibration from the compromised section of the glass where the assassin had crashed. It was weak, but it was there.

A daring, almost suicidal idea formed.

"Misha," Anya whispered, pouring all her will into the Spire device. She wasn't trying to disrupt the Cascade now; she was trying to *connect*. She sent a surge of raw, unchanneled emotional energy, a burst of love and defiance, hoping it would cut through the neurological prison Silas had built.

The Spire device flared, a blinding blue light that pulsed with a desperate, wild intensity. It resonated with Misha's own struggling consciousness, a raw, painful echo of his fight against the implant. For a moment, the entire Glass Maze hummed with the conflicting energies.

Then, the crack in the plasteel wall, already weakened, spider-webbed further, the vibrations from the Spire device finding its fault lines. With a deafening shriek of tearing plasteel, a section of the transparent wall ruptured, sucking out the nerve agent into the vacuum of Veridia's upper atmosphere. The air rushed in, clean and cold, but it was too late. The assassins, caught in the immediate cloud, spasmed, their movements seizing as their neural systems shut down. They collapsed, inert figures in the shattered maze.

Anya gasped, sucking in the fresh air, her body screaming in protest. The Spire device was burning hot in her hand, its power momentarily exhausted. She had cleared a path, but the effort had nearly consumed her.

She pushed herself forward, driven by the thought of Misha. The central core was visible now, a massive, glowing blue pillar at the heart of the Spire. And hooked into it, a terrifying array of machinery surrounding a single, small figure. Misha.

She didn't hesitate. She had come too far. Silas was here. And she would make him pay.

Chapter 43

Silas watched, a grim satisfaction turning to horrified disbelief, as the nerve agent cleared in the Glass Maze, revealing not Anya's lifeless body, but the shattered wall and the inert forms of his elite assassins. His eyes narrowed.

"Impossible," he breathed, his voice a low growl. "She utilized a localized resonance cascade, amplified by the Spire artifact, to target a structural weakness. A brute force application, but... effective. Her Seer lineage is more volatile than predicted."

"Director, her signature is approaching the central core," Thorne stammered, his face pale. "Direct trajectory towards Subject M's chamber!"

Silas felt a surge of cold fury, mixed with a chilling anticipation. She was coming. The final confrontation. He had known she would.

"Seal all internal doors to the central core chamber," Silas commanded, his voice regaining its calm, authoritative tone. "Activate all automated defenses. Prepare for personal engagement. And maintain the Resonance Cascade. Do not allow her to disrupt it further."

He walked to the entrance of Misha's chamber, the vast, circular room dominated by the glowing Zenith Spire core, and Misha, strapped into the amplifying array. Silas stood before the only entrance, a solitary figure in his gleaming white uniform, radiating an aura of absolute control.

Anya burst through the final automated door, its metal groaning under the force of her entry. Her clothes were torn, her face streaked with grime, but her eyes burned with an unyielding fire. She clutched the Spire device, its faint blue light now flickering, unstable.

"Silas!" she snarled, her voice raw with grief and rage. "It ends now. You killed Whisper. You tortured Misha. You tried to enslave an entire city!"

Silas merely smiled, a chilling, condescending expression. "Foolish girl. You mistake defiance for strength. The Cascade is complete, Anya. Veridia is mine. Your futile actions merely highlight the chaotic nature of free will. And your brother... he is merely a tool now. A willing conduit for the city's greater good."

He gestured to the glowing core behind him. "Come, Anya. You are powerful, yes. But untrained. Uncontrolled. Join your brother. Become part of the harmony. Or be extinguished."

Anya didn't answer with words. She lunged, fueled by pure, unadulterated hatred. This wasn't a tactical maneuver; it was an act of vengeance. Silas reacted with surprising speed, producing a compact energy pistol from his belt. He fired.

Anya twisted, the bolt searing past her ear. She closed the distance, ignoring the pain in her ribs, the exhaustion that clawed at her. She brought the Spire device up, not to use its power, but as a blunt weapon.

Silas, confident in his own mastery of technology, anticipated a power surge. He moved to counter. But Anya's attack was primal, unrefined. She slammed the device into Silas's hand, crushing his grip on the pistol. The weapon clattered to the floor.

Silas reeled back, his face contorted in pain and surprise. "Primitive!" he snarled.

Anya pressed her advantage. She had trained for this, for breaking through defenses, for finding the weaknesses in the unyielding. She moved with a blur of motion, striking at joints, at pressure points, the brutal lessons from Seraphina a grim dance of destruction. Silas, for all his intellectual brilliance, was a scientist, not a warrior.

He activated a personal energy shield, a shimmering barrier that flickered around him. Anya slammed against it, the impact jarring her to the bone. But she saw the weakness: a subtle distortion where the shield projector was embedded in his arm.

With a guttural cry, Anya channeled every ounce of her remaining strength, every shred of her grief and fury, into a single, desperate blow. She plunged her fist, not just at his shield, but through the flickering energy, aiming for the projector. The Spire device in her hand flared wildly, amplifying the force, creating a localized resonance that overloaded the shield.

The energy shield shimmered, then burst, sending a shower of sparks. Anya's fist connected with Silas's arm, shattering the projector, driving a bone-jarring impact into his shoulder.

Silas screamed, a sound of agony and disbelief, his perfect control shattering. He stumbled backward, his hand flying to his broken arm, his face contorted in pain and rage. He looked at Anya, hatred burning in his eyes.

"You... you fool! You've doomed them all!" he shrieked, gesturing wildly at Misha and the central core. "The Cascade! It cannot be stopped! You've broken the system!"

But Anya was past reasoning. Her eyes were fixed on Silas, on the man who had taken everything from her. She moved again, grabbing his broken arm, twisting him, forcing him towards the pulsing blue core of the Zenith Spire.

Silas fought, snarling, but his intellectual might was useless against Anya's visceral fury. She dragged him, her hands clamped onto his broken arm, towards the glowing, thrumming heart of the Spire.

"No! You don't understand! The feedback loop! It will destroy Veridia!" Silas shrieked, his voice filled with terror.

Anya ignored him. Her gaze was locked on the glowing blue core, and the array where Misha was strapped. She saw the cables, the intricate wiring, the fragile, dangerous connection.

With a final, desperate surge of strength, Anya shoved Silas, propelled by a primal need for retribution. He stumbled, falling backward, his body slamming into the exposed power conduits of the Zenith Spire's central core.

A blinding flash erupted. The air crackled with uncontrolled energy. Silas screamed, a raw, inhuman sound, as the immense power of the Spire surged through his body. His form spasmed, writhing, before he was consumed in a chaotic cascade of blue light and raw energy. The roar was deafening, the smell of ozone and burnt flesh filling the air.

When the light faded, Silas was gone. Reduced to ash and flickering residue by the very power he sought to control.

Anya stood, panting, her body shaking, the Spire device falling from her numb fingers. The central core of the Zenith Spire pulsed erratically, its stable hum now a chaotic, fluctuating roar. The Resonance Cascade, no longer controlled by Silas, began to unravel.

The monitors around Misha's chamber flickered, the neural readings spiking, then stabilizing, then spiking again. The implant on Misha's neck glowed with an erratic blue light, then flickered, then dimmed. His eyes, though still distant, held a flicker of awareness, a hint of his old self returning.

Anya rushed to him, tearing at the restraints, her hands trembling. The Network's control was breaking.

Chapter 44

Chaos erupted across Veridia. The moment Silas was consumed by the Spire's unleashed energy, the Resonance Cascade, his carefully constructed symphony of control, shattered. The pervasive hum that had lulled the city into quiet compliance vanished, replaced by a jarring cacophony of sound and light.

Public screens flickered violently, displaying distorted images, then going dark. The tranquil, placid expressions on the faces of the citizens shifted, replaced by confusion, then disorientation, then a rising tide of questions and a return of their inherent, vibrant chaos. Traffic lights malfunctioned, causing minor collisions and a flurry of angry shouts. Automated drones, suddenly adrift from the central Network control, spun wildly before crashing.

In the Zenith Spire, the alarms blared incessantly, a harsh counterpoint to the erratic pulsing of the core. Network Enforcers, their connection to Silas severed, their movements no longer precise, stumbled in confusion. The entire monolithic organization began to crumble from within, its unified command structure shattered.

Anya worked frantically, tearing Misha free from the amplifying array. The implant on his neck glowed weakly, then fizzled out. He stirred, his eyes fluttering open, a flicker of recognition passing through the haze.

"Anya?" he whispered, his voice hoarse, his gaze slowly focusing on her. "What... what happened?"

Relief, so profound it was almost painful, washed over Anya. He was back. Her brother was back.

As Network alarms shrieked, Boris's voice, surprisingly clear, crackled over her comm. "Anya! We're picking up massive system failures across the Network! They're in chaos! And Seraphina... she's leading a full assault on Network central command in Sector Prime! She says... 'the city is free for the taking!'"

Anya dragged Misha from the array, supporting his weakened frame. "Misha, we need to move. It's over. Silas is dead."

As they made their way through the now-chaotic corridors of the Zenith Spire, they saw Network Enforcers, not actively fighting, but fleeing, their rigid discipline evaporated. The power structure that had held Veridia captive for so long was imploding.

Below, in the streets of Veridia, the reawakening was messy, violent, and utterly liberating. The tranquil facade shattered, revealing the raw, untamed spirit of the city. Riots erupted in some sectors, fueled by years of suppressed anger and a sudden, disorienting return to individual thought. But in others, people looked around, bewildered, then slowly, tentatively, began to connect, to communicate, to feel again. The silence was broken by laughter, by arguments, by the vibrant, unpredictable pulse of a city finally returned to itself.

Anya guided Misha to a hidden maintenance shaft, the very one she had used to infiltrate the Spire. As they descended, she could feel the city below, a cacophony of reawakened life. It wasn't the perfect harmony Silas had envisioned, but it was real.

CHAPTER 44

It was alive.

She knew the fight wasn't truly over. The Crimson Hand, led by Seraphina, would undoubtedly try to seize power, to fill the vacuum left by the Network. The struggle for Veridia's future would continue, but it would be a struggle of free people, choosing their own path.

Anya helped Misha out into the cool night air, the neon lights of Veridia now pulsing with a renewed, vibrant chaos. Her brother was safe. Silas was dead. Whisper's death had been avenged, her sacrifice not in vain. The city was no longer under a silent, insidious control. It was back to normal, in all its chaotic, vibrant, unpredictable glory. The price of truth had been high, marked by blood and loss, but the lines between justice and vengeance, once so blurred, had finally found a grim clarity. Anya Petrova, the street-smart woman who had simply wanted to save her family, had inadvertently set a city free.

Chapter 45

The weeks that followed Silas's death were a whirlwind of volatile change. The Network, decapitated and decentralized, quickly crumbled. Its automated systems faltered, its vast surveillance grid went dark, its Enforcers, stripped of centralized command, scattered like dust.

The Crimson Hand, true to Seraphina's opportunistic nature, moved swiftly to fill the power vacuum. They seized Network assets, consolidated territory, and began to impose their own brutal brand of order. But this time, it wasn't the sterile, insidious control of Silas. It was open, chaotic, and often violent, but it was also... human. There were choices, arguments, and resistance.

Anya, with Misha at her side, stayed in the shadows, observing. Misha was recovering, slowly regaining his strength, his mind still processing the horrific ordeal. The implant on his neck had gone dormant, a scar and a reminder of Silas's cruelty. Anya, too, was changed. The girl who had once shied from conflict was now a hardened survivor, her movements precise, her senses sharp, her gaze unwavering. The Spire device remained with her, a silent, powerful artifact that no longer felt like a burden, but a part of her.

She had fulfilled her vow. Silas was dead, his vision of forced harmony shattered. Veridia was back to its chaotic, vibrant self, a city of towering neon skyscrapers and stark contrasts, where the struggle for power continued, but now, without the invisible chains of the Resonance Cascade.

Anya knew her fight wasn't over. Seraphina's ambition was a new threat, a different kind of darkness. But Misha was safe. And the people of Veridia, for all their renewed turmoil, were free. They had their voices back, their choices back, their chaos back. And in the heart of that chaos, a new truth would emerge: the fight for justice was never truly over, but sometimes, a single shadow could cast a light long enough to make a difference. Anya Petrova, the Ghost, would continue to watch, to protect, and to fight for the neon shadows of Veridia.

About The Author

Tristyn Barberi is a serving member of the United States Navy who has embarked on a new and exciting adventure: the world of writing. Finding joy and creative expression in crafting stories, Tristyn approaches authorship with the same dedication and discipline honed through naval service. While navigating the demands of military life, Tristyn carves out time to explore imaginative landscapes and bring compelling characters to life, writing purely for the love of it.

Also By Tristyn Barberi

-Neon Shadows
City Of Whispers
City Of Sorrow

www.ingramcontent.com/pod-product-compliance
Lightning Source LLC
LaVergne TN
LVHW092049060526
838201LV00047B/1314